William H. D. Adams

The Land of the Incas and the City of the Sun

the story of Francisco Pizarro and the conquest of Peru

William H. D. Adams

The Land of the Incas and the City of the Sun
the story of Francisco Pizarro and the conquest of Peru

ISBN/EAN: 9783337383183

Printed in Europe, USA, Canada, Australia, Japan

Cover: Foto ©Andreas Hilbeck / pixelio.de

More available books at **www.hansebooks.com**

THE LAND OF THE INCAS

AND

THE CITY OF THE SUN.

*THE STORY OF FRANCISCO PIZARRO
AND THE CONQUEST OF PERU.*

BY

W. H. DAVENPORT ADAMS.

"When fierce Pizarro's legions flew
O'er ravaged fields of rich Peru."
JOSEPH WARTON.

BOSTON:
ESTES AND LAURIAT, PUBLISHERS,
301-305 WASHINGTON STREET.

PREFACE.

IN the following pages I seek to tell the stirring story of the Conquest of Peru. That story does not assume the heroic proportions of the record of the Mexican Conquest; and Pizarro, the conqueror, is, I admit, an inferior figure to Hernando Cortes,—inferior as a commander, a statesman, and an administrator,—inferior in intellectual force and moral power. Yet the story has many romantic and picturesque points, just as Pizarro presents many characteristics which are worthy of analysis and consideration. Moreover, while most historians have done full justice to the great Spaniard who overthrew the brilliant empire of Mexico, and have willingly recognized his noble qualities, the conqueror of Peru has been unfortunate enough to meet with artists who have painted his portrait in the blackest colours. It becomes, therefore, an interesting study to trace his career with fairness, to judge his actions with impartiality, and then to determine whether we can endorse the traditional verdict. I, for one, confess myself unable to do so. I

can find no proof of the ferocity and treachery of which
he has so freely been accused. It seems to me that his
moral calibre was exactly that of his age; that he neither
rose above nor sank below the average standard of his
time and country; that though, like Cortes, he committed
some acts of cruelty, he was by no means a man of a
cruel disposition; that though, like most public men of
his day, he was not too scrupulous in the fulfilment of
engagements, yet, on the whole, he was straightforward
and honest in his policy. I think he was capable of
much generosity towards an enemy, and of sincere attachment to a friend; and it seems to me that in the quarrel
between Almagro and himself, he contrasts very favour-
ably with that impulsive and impetuous soldier. Dr.
Robertson ascribes to him "the address, the craft, and
the dissimulation of a politician," but he does not show
in what actions, or at what periods of his life, Pizarro
exhibited these qualities. Mr. Prescott speaks of "his
perfidious treatment of Almagro." The reader who does
me the honour to peruse the following narrative will judge
for himself whether the American historian's censure has
any foundation.

The principal English writers whom one naturally con-
sults for the life of Pizarro and the conquest of Peru are
Dr. Robertson, Mr. Prescott, and Sir Arthur Helps. I
have availed myself of their lucid ordering of facts, and
their shrewd and sagacious reflections; but I have felt
it necessary to go back to the original authorities in
order to form an honest and intelligent estimate for my
own satisfactoin. The following pages, therefore, assume

to be something more than a compilation from purely
English sources, and will be found, I hope, to present,
in some respects, a new and independent narrative. The
Spanish authorities of most value may be thus enume-
rated: Francisco de Xeres, the secretary of Pizarro,
"Verdadera Relacion de la Conquista." There is a
French translation in the collection of M. Ternaux-
Campans (vol. iv., edit. 1837—1841); but no English
version of this very graphic and interesting chronicle is,
I believe, in existence. Garcilaso de la Vega (the son
of a Spanish cavalier and an Indian mother, the niece
of the Inca Huayna Capac), "Commentarios Reales"
(1609—1616). Of this there is a translation by Rycaut.
It is included also in Purchas's "Pilgrims" (vol. iv.);
and the Hakluyt Society have published an elaborate
edition, under the care of Mr. Clement R. Markham.
Aug. de Zárato, "Historia del Descubrimiento y Conquista de la Provincia del Peru;" this has been trans-
lated into French (Paris, 1746). Fr. Lopez de Gomara,
"Historia General de las Indias" (ed. Barcia, 1749).
Auton. de Herrera, "Historia General de los Hichos de
los Castellanos en las Islas y Tierra Firma de Mar
Oceano" (1601). There is, I believe, an English translation by Stephens. Quintana, "Vidas de Españoles
Celebres." These are the writers whose materials necessarily supply the foundation of all later historians; but
both Mr. Prescott and Sir Arthur Helps have enriched
their respective works by reference to various manu-
scripts; as, for instance, Sir Arthur Helps relies greatly
(perhaps too much so) on the "Carta de Vicento de

Valverdo al Emperador Cárlos Quinto," written at Cuzco in 1539—1541; and Mr. Prescott on Pedro Pizarro's " Descubrimiento y Conquista." They are valuable as "side-lights," but they scarcely affect our general conception of the course of events, or materially modify our judgments upon the men concerned in them.

In conclusion, I may be allowed to express my hope that the concise and comprehensive summary herein attempted will be found of some utility. It has at least the merit of being no servile imitation or repetition of its predecessors.

CONTENTS.

CHAPTER I.

PAGE

PERU AND ITS PEOPLE.—THEIR RELIGION AND
GOVERNMENT 13

CHAPTER II.

EARLY CAREER OF FRANCISCO PIZARRO.—UNDER-
TAKES THE CONQUEST OF PERU . . . 26

CHAPTER III.

THE INVASION.—CAPTURE OF CUZCO, THE CITY
OF THE SUN 74

CHAPTER IV.

DEATH OF ATAHUALPA.—THE SPANISH SETTLE-
MENT 1C7

CHAPTER V.

SIEGE AND RELIEF OF CUZCO 143

CHAPTER VI.

PAGE

THE FEUD BETWEEN ALMAGRO AND PIZARRO.—
EXECUTION OF ALMAGRO 179

CHAPTER VII.

EXPEDITION OF GONZALO PIZARRO, AND DISCOVERY
OF THE RIVER AMAZON. . . . 207

CHAPTER VIII.

ASSASSINATION OF FRANCISCO PIZARRO . . 232

LIST OF ILLUSTRATIONS.

PAGE

THE INCA . . . . *Frontispiece*

PIZARRO AND HIS COMPANIONS COMING IN SIGHT
OF SEVILLE 28

ALTERCATION BETWEEN PIZARRO AND ALMAGRO . 60

STONE IDOL OF THE PERUVIANS 64

CHILICUCHIMA 100

EXECUTION OF ATÁHUALLPA 114

HEROIC DEFENCE OF CUZCO 162

ASSASSINATION OF PIZARRO 246

CHAPTER I.

ON the west coast of the South Pacific Ocean lies Peru, the ancient "land of the Incas." Its western boundary is the State of Ecuador, its northern Bolivia, its eastern the vast empire of Brazil. Geographers estimate its total area at upwards of 500,000 square miles; its extreme length at 1,100 miles; its extreme breadth, in the north, at 780 miles, diminishing in the south to fifty or sixty miles. Its coast line, owing to its numerous sinuosities, exceeds 1,700 miles; but for the greater part is represented by steep and lofty cliffs, at the foot of which the billows of the Pacific incessantly thunder; and consequently the harbours are few, and, with the exception of those of Callao and Paita, neither very commodious nor very secure. The distinguishing physical feature of the country, determining its character, climate, and resources, is the immense mountain system of the Andes, which traverses its entire extent. This system divides the surface into three distinct regions, varying in temperature, in products, and in scenery. First, there is the Littoral, or coast region, which rises from the shore to the base of the mountains; arid, sandy, and irregular, except where it is preserved in the deep rich valleys, excavated and enriched by streams descending from the Cordilleras. The tracts lying between these green oases are covered with a fine yellow sand, which the wind frequently raises in huge columns of from seventy to eighty feet in height, and hurries over the sun-burnt soil. No rain falls in the greater part of the Littoral. The south-east trade winds, after passing over the Atlantic, cross the wide forest-lands of Brazil, and fertilize them with abundant showers; but their vapour is taken up and condensed by the heights of the Cordilleras, which they crown with diadems of snow, and they reach the Peruvian coast dry, cool, and pungent. At night, however, the dews are ample and refreshing.

From the Littoral we ascend to the Sierra, the mountainous belt which intervenes between the western base of the maritime Cordillera and the eastern base of the eastern Cordillera; in other words, it includes the two ranges, or Cordilleras, of the Andes, over a breadth of a hundred miles. These are connected by transverse chains, and present every diversity of mountain scenery. The eastern range, or Andes proper, attains its greatest elevation towards the south ; the western range dominates towards the north. Both are conspicuous for towering peaks, which rise to a loftier altitude than Mont Blanc; for lofty table-lands, which rejoice in an invigorating air, and wave with prodigal harvests of wheat and maize, and rye and barley ; for green valleys and shady hollows, which teem with heliotrope and lupine, fuchsia, salvia, and calceolaria, rich in spontaneous growth. They do not, however, present that profuse fertility of vegetation which is characteristic of the Himalaya, nor are they so rich in animal life. The puma, or American lion, wanders among their solitudes ; the lammergeir and the vulture haunt their loftier summits ; the llama, the guanaco, and the vicuña roam about their green sides and their sheltered valleys. The principal peaks are Sahama, 22,350 feet ; Parinacota, 22,030 ; Gualatieri, 21,900 ; Pomarape, 21,900; Cerequipa (a volcano), 20,320; Chipicani, 19,745; Quenuta, 18,765 ; Coloro, 17,930; Apu Cunaranu, 17.950 ; and Vilcañoto, 17,525. The more remarkable table-lands are the plain of Titicaca, in the centre of which lies the great lake of Titicaca, at an elevation of 12,846 feet ; the knot of Cuzco, where several mountain-chains converge, and with their grand barriers enclose a delightful area of tropical valleys and luxuriant forests ; and the knot of Pasco, the average altitude of which is 8,000 feet.

These and other table-lands yield luxuriant crops of every European grain, and are frequently dotted with populous towns and thriving villages. Nor is this a modern condition of things; for centuries prior to the Spanish conquest these table-lands were inhabited by a mysterious aboriginal race, bearing the same relation to the Incas and the present inhabitants as the Etruscans bear to the ancient Etruscans and the Italians of our own days.

The third region, the Montaña, occupying two-thirds of the entire surface of the country, extends for some hundreds of miles to the dubious and undefined boundaries of Brazil. The Amazon forms its northern boundary; Bolivia, its southern. Alluvial plains here alternate with immense tracts of virgin forest, where animal and vegetable life, unshackled by man, literally runs riot. The virgin soil, never harassed by plough or harrow, is of an amazing fertility. In the neighbourhood of the chief streams are occasional farms, but, as a whole, this boundlessly fertile region awaits the coming of the agriculturist. The forests consist of huge trees, some remarkable for the beauty of their foliage, others for the excellence of their timber; some for their fruit and flowers, others for their odoriferous gums and resins. Luxurious parasites and creepers climb up their trunks and festoon their branches, and, springing from one to another, weave everywhere an almost impenetrable network, through which may be seen the flash of brightly coloured wings. The trees attain an enormous stature, frequently to 120 and 150 feet, and their girth is proportionate. Immense ferns and brilliant orchids thrive among the rank under-growth at their feet. In the deeper sylvan recesses the heat is necessarily suffocating, for no refreshing breezes ever make their way through the dense overhanging canopy of greenness; while, after the periodical rains, the moisture is so excessive that it rises like a thick mist among the huge stems of the trees, and floats suspended like a mountain-cloud.

A silence like that of the grave prevails in the leafy wilderness during the day, but at sunset all the voices of nature seem released from a magic charm, and bird and beast simultaneously unite in what we may assume to be a farewell chorus to the departing luminary. The night is not less solemn in its hush than the day, but at the first burst of dawn animal life is again stirred by one common impulse. Occasionally, indeed, some nocturnal prowler awakens a transient alarm, which spreads from bough to bough and tree to tree, until all the forest echoes with the clamour. More dreadful is the hurly-burly when the storm-wind rushes on its furious path : then, in its furious violence, the green tops of the trees are swayed to and fro like reeds ; the darkness of midnight descends upon the scene ; the streams, swollen by the rains, roar through the resounding glades ; the vivid shafts of light-ning reveal the nests of terror-stricken animals, scattering in headlong flight through the forest depths, and by each successive thunder peal moved with renewed panic.

Such is a brief outline of the physical geography of Peru. West of the Andes it has no important rivers ; to the east, its great streams, the Marañon, the Yucayali, the

Purus, and the Huallaga, belong to the vast water-system of the Amazons. Its vegetable products are so various as to defy enumeration; its mineral resources have greatly fallen off, but still include silver, lead, copper, and some gold. The silver mines of Potosi once enjoyed a world-wide reputation : they are comprised within the boundaries of Bolivia. Guano, and nitrate of soda and borax, are now among the principal articles of Peruvian export.

The origin of the name of Peru is unknown; nor are we well acquainted with its earlier annals. Roughly speaking, its history divides into three distinct eras—the pre-Incarial, the period of the Incas, and the modern or Spanish period. Of the pre-Incarial, the chief records are the mighty ruins of Tia-Huanacu, on the shore of Lake Titicaca; consisting of colossal idols, of huge pillars, like those at Stonehenge, of masses of hewn stone, and sculptured monolithic gateways. Some remains may also be seen at Paclacamac, near Laina, where, at the epoch of the Peruvian invasion, a gorgeous temple existed without any image or visible symbol of a god. It was raised in honour of a mysterious deity, Pachacamar, or the Earth-beater; and no other deity seems to have been worshipped by the pre-Incarial race.

The beginning of the second period is shrouded in mystery. But all conquering races have loved to claim for themselves a divine original, and the Incarial Peruvians in their traditions go back to one Manco Capac, who, with his wife, Manca Ocollo, first presented themselves on the shores of Lake Titicaca, declaring that they were children of Cuti, or the Sun, and commissioned by that glorious power to teach the ways of light and sweetness to the native population. Manco carried in his hand a wedge, or wand, of gold; and announced that wherever this wedge, or wand, on being struck upon the ground, should sink into the earth, and disappear, the Sun had commanded him to build his capital city. The pre-destined spot proved to be the plain of Cuzco, and there Manco Capac, the first Inca, founded the city of Cuzco. He proceeded to instruct his followers in the rudiments of industry and in the arts of social life. He established a simple and humane legislation, and ordained that no man should have more than one wife. The religion which he inculcated centred in a worship of the Sun as the vivifier of the heavens and the dispenser of all the benefits of nature; and he founded a religious community of virgins who ministered in the national temples. Meanwhile, Manca Ocollo taught the women to sew and spin and weave, and to lead pure and virtuous lives; and the infant state flourished in such tranquil prosperity under the wise rule of those remarkable individuals, that it gradually drew towards it large numbers of the aborigines. Before the death of Manco, thirteen towns had risen to the east, and thirty to the west of Cuzco.

After a reign of thirty or forty years, Manco, finding that the end was at hand, assembled his principal subjects, introduced his son and successor, and exhorted them to preserve with reverent care the laws and institutions to which they owed their happiness. He specially urged upon them the duty of zealously maintaining their

religious creed, and reminded his son that he was not
only the ruler but the high priest of his people. Sinchi
Roca, who ascended the throne about 1062, was of a
martial disposition, and added to his inheritance by
conquest. Succeeding Incas witnessed the rapid exten-
sion of the Peruvian kingdom by the attractive influence
of its prosperity. About 1453, the eleventh of the
dynasty, Tupac Inca Yupanqui, led his army southward,
crossed the great desert of Atacanca, and pushed his
southern frontier as far as the river Maule (in lat. 36° S.)
On his return he boldly crossed the Chilian Andes, and
by a difficult and dangerous route marched back to
Cuzco in triumph. Meanwhile, his son, Huayna Capac,
had led an army northward, crossed the Amazon, and
subdued the kingdom of Quito. He ascended the throne
in 1475, and under him the empire of the Incas reached
its meridian splendour, stretching from the tropic forests
of the Amazon to the temperate plains of Chili, and
from the sources of the Paraguay to the shores of the
Pacific. The centre and capital of this great territory
was Cuzco (*i.e.* "the navel"), whence, to the borders of
the kingdom, branched off four great highways, north
and south, and east and west, each traversing one of the
four provinces, or viceroyalties, into which Peru was
divided. The main road ran from Quito, through Cuzco,
into the recesses of Chili ; crossing rivers and chasms
upon bridges of plaited osiers, winding up steep precipitous ascents, and piercing in tunnels the solid rock.
It was nearly two thousand miles in length ; its average
breadth was twenty feet ; and it was paved with flags of

freestone. At intervals of five miles it was studded with posts, or small buildings, to each of which was attached a small staff of runners, for the swift conveyance of official despatches.

The government of the Incas was a paternal despotism, a mild and prudent theocracy. The Inca, as representative of the race, was the head of the priesthood, and presided over all religious festivals. He was the legislator, the admin'strator, the source of all power and honour. He levied taxes, and commanded the army. His insignia of royalty was a peculiar head-dress, with a tasselled fringe, and two feathers placed in it erect. The religion which he taught was remarkable, in contradistinction to that of Mexico, for its humane and gentle character. The altar of the Sun was stained by no human sacrifices; the offerings heaped upon it were plants and cereals, fruits and milk, and, on special occasions, a lamb, or sheep, or goat. Such a religion necessarily had its effect on the character of the people, who, though under some of their Incas they accomplished considerable conquests, were, on the whole, of a pacific disposition. Their single cruel custom was one which probably arose in the intimate connection existing between the Inca and his people. When an Inca died, a large number of persons suffered death—voluntarily, it would seem,—in order that he might not enter the other world without a retinue suitable to his rank.

Social distinctions in Peru partook of the primitive simplicity of the government. The land was divided into three portions, one of which was consecrated to the

Sun, a second to the Inca, while the third belonged to the People. The first share sufficed for the erection of temples, the maintenance of the priesthood, and the support of public worship. The second defrayed the cost of the royal household and the expenditure upon government purposes. The third was annually allotted among the people in proportion to the rank and numbers of each family. All three divisions were cultivated by the people, who were summoned to their daily task by an officer appointed for the purpose. Their work was lightened by the sound of musical instruments, and the singing of the national songs and ballads. The manufactures of the country and the mines were wrought on the same principle, each person giving a certain portion of time, during which he was supported at the government expense, to the needs of the Sun and the Inca. This system seems to have been attended with some beneficial results : the idea of mutual help and community of interest naturally stimulated a feeling of kindred, and strengthened the bonds of humanity. The Peruvians formed one great family, actuated by the same sympathies, and labouring for the same object. On the other hand, it tended to depress them all to the same level, to impede the progress of civilization, to prevent the development of intellectual vigour, and to crush individual effort and ambition.

Agriculture was the chief concern and occupation of the Peruvians, but they gave a portion of their energies to the cultivation of the arts necessary for the support and comfort of life. A word or two may be said as to their mode of building. This varied, necessarily, with the various climatic conditions of the country: beneath a tropical sky, only the lightest tenements were required, but in the colder districts solidity and strength of construction were carefully observed. Their houses, made of sun-burned bricks, were square, about eight feet high, and windowless. The palaces of the Incas and the mansions of the nobles were on a somewhat larger scale, and in the interior were lavishly decorated with plates and bosses of silver and gold, and with figures of plants and animals in the same metals. The Temple of the Sun, at Cuzco, called Coricancha, or " Place of Gold," excelled in magnificence any other building in the empire. On the western wall, facing the eastern portal, was a gorgeous representation of the orb of day, consisting of a colossal human face in gold, with golden rays emanating from it in every direction; while all around the building blazed with golden plates and bands, and golden cornices and images, which, when the sunshine fell upon them, shone with an almost intolerable intensity of splendour.

The ingenuity of the Peruvians was also shown in other departments of human labour. They not only wrought in gold and silver, but they manufactured and polished mirrors of shining stones. They had earthen utensils of various forms and sizes, and also different kinds of instruments. In ornamental articles they displayed considerable dexterity and taste ; and considering their want of proper tools, and the fact that they knew nothing of the use of iron, their perseverance and patience must have been exemplary. Yet in these respects, as in their character and government, they were far inferior to the Mexicans; their civilization was of a primitive and unprogressive type. As they were under their first Inca, so were they under their twelfth ; and, had the empire survived, so would they have been under their twenty-fourth. They might multiply and extend, but their social system forbade that they should rise. In such a system reform was impossible; immobility was the very condition of its existence ; the first external or internal shock must necessarily involve it in utter ruin. It has been well said that if the gentleness of the natives, and their implicit obedience to the laws of the Incas, had been the means of advancing them some few steps forward in civilization, these very circumstances militated in other respects against their further advancement in social life. In Peru, as elsewhere, a "paternal despotism" meant "popular enervation." The moral energies were sapped and undermined by that kind of lifeless domesticity which found neither stimulus for emulation nor necessity for exertion. Satisfied with the mode of living they had inherited, and a mode of living supposed to be approved by their deity, they never dreamed of, never yearned after, a higher order of things. Moreover, they were bred in so absolute a conviction of the surpassing superiority of the Incas, that they were averse to all kinds of speculation. To criticise was irreverent; to doubt, profane. The superiority of the prince's judgment being acknowledged by all his subjects, they never felt inclined to investigate his infallibility. The reasoning faculties were thus suffered to rust unused ; while the comparative social comfort and actual tranquillity which the Peruvians enjoyed satisfied them so completely, that they never desired anything better. How could they pine for what had never been presented to them? We repeat, then, that though in amenity and the softer aspects of life superior to the Mexicans, they were in all essential respects, and in all the higher motives and purposes of national existence, inferior.

Such was Peru and the Peruvians when they first became known to Europeans. The first white man landed on the Pacific coast in 1516, or two years before the death of Huayna Capac; but the storm of conquest did not break upon Peru until sixteen years later. The reigning Inca was then Huascar, son of Huayna Capac who was engaged in hostilities with his brother Atahualpa, to whom had been bequeathed the kingdom of Quito. This intestine conflict greatly facilitated, as we shall see, the conquest of Peru by the Spaniards.

CHAPTER II.

OWARDS the close of the fifteenth century was born at Trujillo, a considerable town in Spain, Francisco Pizarro. His father, Gonzalo Pizarro, was a cavalier of high birth and good estate, who had won distinct'on in the wars. His mother was a peasant woman, with no attraction but her personal beauty, who, it is said, gave birth to her son on the bare stone steps of a church, and then took him to her squalid hovel to share her poverty and shame. As an illegitimate child, Pizarro, though he bore his father's name, was never recognized by him, never admitted to his presence, never allowed any portion of his wealth. He was denied even the merest rudiments of education, so that he could neither read nor write; and when he emerged from childhood was placed in the low occupation of a swineherd. There was in him, however, a natural force of character, an inherent energy of intellect, which would not be denied ; and, indeed, a meaner spirit might have rebelled against the harsh conditions of his lot, against the scanty rations of coarse food, the bed of straw on a paved floor, the menaces and blows which • were his daily portion. The blood of the Pizarros had in it a hot, impetuous, masterful strain; and this his father had conferred upon him, though he had denied him his love and protection. When he was about fifteen years old, and chafing more and more bitterly against the yoke he bore, Trujillo was visited by an old wave-worn, storm-beaten sailor, who had sailed with Columbus on his ever-famous expedition of discovery. He was as well pleased to talk as Pizarro was to listen, and into the boy's ears poured a stirring tale of the adventures he had undergone and the sights he had seen. He told him how for many days and nights the great Genoese seaman had led them across a shoreless sea, with nothing visible but the heavens above and the waters all around; how the hearts of himself and his comrades had sunk within them as they receded farther and farther from their native land and plunged into a vast and apparently illimitable waste ; how at last they were cheered by the welcome signs of strange birds perching in the rigging, and strange plants and fragments of wood floating on the waves; how, one night, the keen eye of their leader detected the flash of a light, like that of a torch or lantern, moving in the dark obscurity before them ; how, next morning, the sailor at the mast-top made the air ring with the joyous shout of "Land ahead!" and how that land had proved to be a bounteous shore, teeming with Nature's choicest products, and rich, it was believed, in gold and silver and precious stones, of which any man might have his share who carried thither a brave heart and a ready sword.

So romantic a story did not fail to appeal to that love of adventure which had hitherto lain dormant in the young swineherd's nature. His eyes glowed and his blood ran wildly while he mused upon what he had heard, and contrasted the fair fortunes of the men who crossed the seas to those new and wondrous regions with his own dull and uneventful lot. He resolved on the earliest opportunity to abandon Trujillo and its ignominy, and, if he could not join some expedition bound for "far Cathay," to enter the Spanish army, and woo destiny as a soldier. He communicated his intention to two of his young companions, swineherds like himself; and the three contrived one night to elude the vigilance of their master, and, stealing out of Trujillo, fared forth on foot for Seville. The way was long and painful; though to Pizarro, who had a vivid imagination, there was doubtless an infinite source of pleasure in the various scenery through which they passed ; the forest shades of oak and chestnut, the glossy groves of olives, the breadths of corn-field waving with a coming harvest, the bright brook sparkling through the verdant pastures, the vineyards blooming with the purple of their ripening clusters. They traversed the Guadalupe Mountains, obtaining a night's shelter and a frugal breakfast in the hut of a kindly shepherd, who, after hearing Pizarro's eager anticipations of future fame, naïvely said, as he bade him farewell, " God prosper you ! and when you become a great cap'ain, remember the night you spent under the shep-

Pizarro and his Companions coming in sight of Seville.

herd's roof." In due time they crossed the wide and noble
Guadiana, and entered the ancient town of Merida, which
sleeps in the shadow of its stately castle, unmindful of the
gay processions of cavaliers that once thronged its streets;
unmindful of the Roman legionaries once garrisoned
there by the Emperor Trajan. The ascent of the Sierra
Morena was next accomplished; then they gradually
descended into fertile and vine-clad valleys, and through
a landscape of picturesque beauty pressed on to
Seville.

A tall, robust lad of fifteen, with a well-knit frame, a
quick eye, and an air of activity and daring, Francisco
Pizarro quickly obtained admission to the ranks of the
Spanish army. After a brief period of training, he was
despatched with his battalion to join the forces then in
Italy under Gonsalvo de Cordova, the " Great Captain,"
who was fighting to restore King Ferdinand to the throne
of Naples. Pizarro was present at several engagements
with the French, and attracted the favourable notice of
his superiors by his splendid courage, his promptitude of
action, and his faculty of endurance. After the capture
of Naples, and the expulsion of the French, the Spanish
army returned home, and Pizarro was rewarded by pro-
motion to the rank of lieutenant. We cannot doubt
that the military experience he gained in Italy proved of
vast service to him in the great enterprise to which he devoted his later life ; and there, too, he acquired that knowledge of men and manners essential to one who purposes
to become a leader of men. He remained in the army for
several years ; but when the prospect of active service

faded away, he began to find the monotony of barrack-
life intolerable. He was before all things a man of
action ; to his quick, aspiring spirit rest was torture; and
we may naturally conclude that his lack of education,
and consequent inability to engage his eager, strenuous
intellect in study, made the uniform dulness of parade
and drill all the harder to bear. The tales which circu-
lated throughout Spain of the treasures of the New
World lying open to every comer, revived the impression
made on his boyish mind by the story of the old follower
of Columbus. The thirst for wealth and power which
had infected half the youth of Spain, he felt as keenly as
any ; and happy was he when at last he obtained a place
in an expedition bound for Hispaniola, then the gate of
the Western Indies. He found himself there among
men with a love of adventure as fervent as his own, and
a courage scarcely less indomitable. Yet it was not long
before the masterfulness, so to speak, of Pizarro's character asserted itself, and he came to be regarded as one
who would faithfully follow and gallantly lead. He stood
out among his companions as gifted with greater foresight,
a sterner purpose, and a stronger will. About 1509 there
arrived in St. Domingo two Spanish cavaliers, to each of
whom had been given as his government a portion of the
mainland of the Isthmus of Darien. These were Alonzo de
Ojeda and Diego da Nicuesa. To prevent collision between
their interests and partisans, they agreed that the river
Darien should be the boundary line between their respective provinces; between Urabá, which was Ojeda's, and
extended eastward to Cape de la Vela ; and Veragua,

which was Nicuesa's, and extended westward to Cape Gracias à Dios. This agreement concluded, Ojeda prepared to take possession of his province, collected a little army, and invited Pizarro to accompany him as second in command. He gladly assented, and on the 10th of November, 1509, Ojeda and his lieutenant sailed from the fort of St. Domingo with two ships, two brigantines, three hundred men, and twelve horses.

In four or five days Ojeda reached the place which the Spaniards had named Carthagena, and setting aside the warning of Juan de la Cosa, one of his officers, who had visited the coast before, and knew that the Indians were not friendly, resolved to disembark. Taking Juan de la Cosa with him, because of his knowledge of the country, he attacked the Indian town or village of Calunar, and made seventy prisoners. Flushed with success, he marched against the large town of Turbaco, and finding it deserted, went in swift pursuit of its fugitive inhabitants. But not keeping his men together, they were exposed to a sudden assault from the Indians, who drove them back to the shore, and with volleys of poisoned arrows slaughtered the whole detachment except Ojeda and another. Ojeda took refuge in the woods, where, next day, a party of his men found him, speechless with hunger, but with his red sword still in his hand, and the dents, it is said, of three hundred arrows in his shield. Soon afterwards, Nicuesa's fleet hove in sight, and the two governors joining company, they landed a force of four hundred men to punish the Indians for defending their native country. Turbaco was burnt to the ground, and its unfortunate inhabitants—men, women, and children—killed.

Nicuesa then sailed for his own province, and Ojeda made for the Gulf of Urabá, where he landed on the eastern side, and on a commanding eminence founded a town, to which he gave the name of St. Sebastian. He then sent his Indian prisoners, and the plunder of Calunar and Turbaco, to St. Domingo, in order to obtain more men and supplies. But, with the usual improvidence of these Spanish adventurers, he had taken no thought about feeding his men, and in a few days, having exhausted their scanty stores, and being unable to obtain any from the hostile Indians, he and his company suffered all the anguish of famine. Happily there arrived off the coast a vessel which its commander, Bernardino de Talavera, had stolen from the Genoese, and the bread and meat and wine which he had collected Ojeda eagerly bought. Ojeda seems to have been deficient in most of the qualifications of a successful leader; but at all events he was a cavalier of courage, and in repelling the attacks of the Indians he was always one of the foremost. Noting his temerity, they beguiled him into an ambuscade, and poured in upon him their poisoned arrows, one of which wounded him in the thigh. Such wounds were generally considered mortal; but Ojeda determined on acting as his own surgeon, and invented a remedy which would have tested the fortitude of a Stoic. Two plates of iron, heated to a white heat, he bound on to his thigh, and yet he refrained from even a groan! His leg and thigh were shrunken by the torture, and the heat so inflamed his body that it was found necessary to expend a pipe of vinegar in moistening the bandages which were afterwards applied.

The supplies brought by Talavera were now exhausted, and famine again laid its grasp upon the warriors at St. Sebastian. It was evident to Ojeda that all would perish, unless he returned to Hispaniola for recruits and provisions. He appointed Pizarro governor in his absence, and informed him and his people that if he did not return within fifty days they would be free to abandon the settlement, embark on board the two brigantines, and go where they would. He then set sail, but saw the American coast no more. At St. Domingo he could obtain no assistance, and some time afterwards died neglected and in extreme want. For fifty dreary days Pizarro waited, watching night and morning for the expected sai's, living upon palm nuts and the flesh of wild hogs, and losing many of his men through disease and the poisoned shafts of the Indians. As the two brigantines would not hold all his company, he was forced to wait until death had reduced them to the required number. Then, having killed and salted the surviving horses for food, he embarked in one of the vessels, placing a man named Vahuzuela in charge of the other.

They were scarce twenty leagues from the shore when Vahuzuela's crazy craft—struck, it was supposed, by some large fish—sunk suddenly. Pizarro, reserved for a great destiny, sailed on to Carthagena, where he fell in with the Bachiller Enciso, Ojeda's alcalde mayor, who, in ignorance of his master's fate, was wandering in search of him with one hundred and fifty men, several horses, arms, powder, and provisions. He cou d hardly be persuaded that Pizarro and his followers had not deserted Ojeda, and at first was disposed to put them in prison ; but their wan faces and meagre bodies were powerful witnesses to the truth of their story. Pizarro would have dissuaded him from going to St. Sebastian, but the Bachiller Enciso was resolute to fulfil what he conceived to be his duty, and they all set sail. Just as he neared St. Sebastian, his vessel struck on a rock and was dashed to p'eces : those on board saved themselves, but lost their cattle and provisions. On getting ashore, they found the fortress entirely destroyed, and were soon reduced to extremities as miserable as those which Pizarro and his party had previously suffered. In this conjuncture, a certain adventurer and brilliant swordsman, named Vasco Nuñez de Balboa, informed the sufferers that once before he had visited this Gulf of Uabá, but that he had landed on the western shore, where a great river flowed through a fertile country; and he added that as the Indians there did not make use of poisoned arrows, he advised that they should all make their way thither without delay.

His advice was so far adopted that the Bachiller Enciso, with Vasco Nuñez and a hundred men, set out for the said river, which is now known as the Darien. They reached it in safety, but found the Indians hostilely inclined, and fought with them a great battle, in which all the loss was on the side of the hapless Indians, whose innoxious arrows availed little against the arms and armour of the

Spaniards. In an Indian town close by they obtained a large supply of provisions, and much booty in gold. So Enciso sent for the rest of his company from St. Sebastian, and founded on the bank of the broad bright river the town of Santa Maria de la Antigua del Darien. He lacked the vigour, however, necessary for one who would be a ruler of men. His community split into three factions ; one remaining loyal to himself, another declaring for Balboa, and the third for Nicuesa. Eventually the three came to an agreement to invite the last-named to become governor, and sent deputies to him for that purpose. Nicuesa was a man of hasty temper and scanty prudence, and while accepting the invitation, he declared that as the town of Darien lay within the boundaries of his own province (which was true), he should confiscate whatever gold Ojeda's men had acquired there. The deputies hastened to make known this saying, and much also concerning Nicuesa which they had gathered from his followers, to the Darienites. They quickly repented of the choice they had made, and, instigated by Balboa, prepared to receive him as no invited governor was ever received before. On his arrival, he found the shore lined with armed men, who, when he attempted to land, bade him in no courteous terms return to his own settlement. He persevered, and next day was actually allowed to disembark ; but they speedily seized upon him, and turned him adrift, with seventeen faithful comrades, in the craziest bark they could find. It was on the 1st of March, 1511, that he put out to sea, and he was never again heard of.

The virtual ruler of Darien was now Vasco Nuñez de Balboa, and to make his authority secure, he insisted that Enciso should leave the settlement, either for Hispaniola or Castile, as he liked best. Thereafter he ruled with a firm hand, but not tyrannically. Hearing from some Indians that gold was to be found at Cueva, about thirty leagues distant, he sent Pizarro with six men to explore the district. Half-way the natives, under one Cunaco, fell upon the little band. Had they used poisoned arrows, none could have escaped; but their shafts did not slay, though they inflicted severe wounds; and Pizarro fought with such splendid courage that he put them to flight, and killed many, before he returned to Darien. Balboa then set out with a hundred men to carry fire and sword through the Indian province; but all its inhabitants had fled, and he could find not a single victim. He next turned his arms against Careta, the Cacique of Cueva, whose town he captured and plundered, while the chief and his family he carried prisoners to Darien. Wisely treating him with lenity, Balboa gained in him a valuable ally, and entered into an agreement by which he undertook to grow supplies for the Spaniards on condition that they assisted him in his war against a chief named Poncha.

This pact was duly carried out, and afterwards Balboa extended his friendly relations to another Indian Cacique, named Comogre, the ruler of a territory called Comogra, on the sea-coast. Balboa paid him a visit, was hospitably entertained, and presented with seventy slaves and 4,000 peros of gold. Some dispute arising in reference to its division, Comogre's son exclaimed, "How is it Christians, that you quarrel for so small a thing as this? If you have so keen a lust for gold that in order to obtain it you trouble and disquiet the peaceful nations of these lands, and, enduring all kinds of pain and labour, banish yourselves from your own homes, I will show you a country where you may satisfy your thirst. But for this purpose it is necessary that you should be more in number than you are now, for you would have to fight your way against powerful princes, foremost among whom is the King Jubanania, whose country, abounding in gold, is distant from our country six suns." He added that this country lay towards a great sea, and southwards; and this was the earliest information which the Spaniards obtained of Peru and the Pacific.

It was not Balboa's fortune, however, to reach the golden land of the Incas, though he lived to see the vast ocean which washed its rocky coast. Some months elapsed—months spent in adventure and exploration of which I have no space to sum up the record; after which, receiving from Hispaniola a reinforcement of a hundred and fifty men, and his appointment as Captain-General, he undertook the daring enterprise of searching for the Southern Sea. His little army consisted of a hundred and ninety well-armed men; he took a number of slaves to act as porters, and several bloodhounds. Francisco Pizarro accompanied him as second in command. They left Darien early in September, 1513; went by sea to Careta's territory; crossed into that of Poncha, whom he conciliated by presents of trinkets, looking-

glasses, and hatchets; and then began the ascent of the
mountain range that, traversing the isthmus, links together
the Rocky Mountains of the northern division of the continent with the Andes of the southern division. Entering
the country of a chief named Quanqua, they found the
Indians arrayed in battle to oppose them; but the fire-
arms of the Spaniards put them to a bloody rout. So
great was the slaughter that the field reminded those who
saw it of the shambles.

At Quanqua's town, or village, Balboa left his invalided
men, and taking with him some Indians as guides, he
continued his laborious ascent of the rugged sierras.
On the 25th of September, 1513, he was near the summit
of a peak from which, so the Indians told him, the great
southern ocean was visible. Halting his soldiers, Balboa
went forth a one to ascend the topmost height; and, first
of the men of the old world, looked out upon the vast
Pacific, which, in the course of years, was to be furrowed
by the great commercial highways of nations. Having
gazed his fill upon the shining waters, he called to his
men to come up; and Pizarro was the second to stand
upon the airy summit. Balboa then addressed his
soldiers: "You see here, cavaliers and children mine,
how our desires are being fulfilled, and that the end
of our labours approaches. That, indeed, we ought
to accept as certain; for as all that King Comogre's
son told us of this sea has proved to be true, so
I feel assured will all that he has told us of incom-
parable treasures in it. God and His blessed Mother,
through whose help we have come hither to behold

this sea, will favour us that we may enjoy all that it contains." *

Sir Arthur Helps, in reference to this remarkable incident, which forms one of the landmarks in the world's history, observes that " every great and original action has a perspective greatness, not alone from the thoughts of the man who achieves it, but from the various aspects and high thoughts which the same action

* This notable episode in the annals of discovery touched the imagination of Keats, and in one of his sonnets he has a fine reference to it, though he unfortunately confuses Cortes, the conqueror of Mexico, with Nuñez de Balbao :—

> " Like stout Cortez when with eagle eyes
> He stared at the Pacific, and all his men
> Looked at each other with a wild surmise,
> Silent, upon a peak in Darien."

It has also suggested a fine stirring ballad by Mr. Buchanan Read :—

> " From San Domingo's crowded wharf
> Fernandez' vessel bore,
> To seek in unknown lands afar
> The Indian's golden ore ;
> And hid among the freighted casks,
> Where none might see or know,
> Was one of Spain's immortal men,
> Three hundred years ago !

> " But when the fading town and land
> Had dropped below the sea,
> He met the captain face to face,
> And not a fear had he !
> ' What villain thou ?' Fernandez cried,
> ' And wherefore serve us so ?'
> ' To be thy follower,' he replied,
> Three hundred years ago.

will continue to present and call up in the minds of
others to the end, it may be, of all time. And so," he
adds, "a remarkable event may go on acquiring more and
more significance. In this case, our knowledge that the
Pacific, which Vasco Nuñez then beheld, occupies more
than one-half of the earth's surface, is an element of
thought which in our minds lightens up and gives an
awe to this first gaze of his upon those mighty waters.
To him the scene might not at that moment have suggested
much more than it would have done to a mere con-

> " He wore a manly form and face,
>   A courage firm and bold ;
> His words fell on his comrades' hearts
>   Like precious drops of gold.
> They saw not his ambitious soul ;
>   He spoke it not—for, lo !
> He stood among the common ranks
>   Three hundred years ago.
>
> " But when Fernandez' vessel lay
>   At golden Darien,
> A murmur, born of discontent,
>   Grew loud among the men :
> And with the word there came the act ;
>   And with the sudden blow
> They raised Balboa from the ranks,
>   Three hundred years ago.
>
> " And while he took command beneath
>   The banner of his lord,
> A mighty purpose grasped his soul,
>   As he had grasped the sword.
> He saw the mountain's fair blue height
>   Whence golden waters flow ;
> Then with his men he scaled the crags,
>   Three hundred years ago.

queror ; indeed, Peter Martyr likens Vasco Nuñez to Hannibal showing Italy to his soldiers." It seems to us that the writer misconceives the effect which the view of the Pacific, as it lay before him in the noontide glow like a huge shield of burnished silver, must have had on the imagination of Balboa. He did not know its vast dimensions ; but he knew at least that it was a mighty sea, and the very vagueness of his knowledge would invest it with the greater sublimity. A strange romance attached to the world's oceans in those credulous

> " He led them up through tangled brakes,
> The rivulet's shining bed,
> And through the storm of poisoned darts
> From many an ambush shed.
> He gained the turret crag—alone,
> And wept ! to see below
> An ocean boundless and unknown,
> Three hundred years ago.
>
> " And while he raised upon that height
> The banner of his lord,
> The mighty purpose grasped him still,
> As still he grasped the sword.
> Then down he rushed with all his men,
> As headlong rivers flow,
> And plunged breast-deep into the sea,
> Three hundred years ago.
>
> " And while he held above his head
> The conquering flag of Spain.
> He waved his gleaming sword, and smote
> The waters of the main.
> For Rome ! for Leon ! and Castile !
> Thrice gave the cleaving blow ;
> And thrice Balboa claimed the sea,
> Three hundred years ago."

days ; and Balboa would look upon the Pacific with wild dreams of marine monsters, of enchanted islands, of mysterious music, passing through his brain. With these would mingle even wilder dreams of golden shores which lay ready to yield up their opulence to the adventurer's sword ; while, like a true Spaniard, he would not fail to think of ignorant peoples to be included in the Spanish empire, and converted to the religion of the Cross.

After his brief oration to his men, Balboa hastened to take formal possession, on behalf of his sovereign, of the Pacific and all that was in it, and with cairns of stones and crosses made of the trunks and branches of trees he raised memorials of the event. He then pushed forward into the territory of an Indian chief called Chiapes, who at first attempted resistance, but was quickly defeated, and afterwards, according to Balboa's statesmanlike fashion, conciliated, and made a friend of. Balboa, like Columbus, was careful, so far as circumstances allowed, to treat the Indians humanely, and to gain their confidence ; there is less blood upon his fame than upon that of any of the Spanish conquerors, and he was second only to Cortes in political sagacity. Thus he loaded the Indian guides whom he had brought from Quanqua's country with presents, and sent them back in safety—a mode of procedure which secured the confidence of those whom he hired from Chiapes. Before he resumed his march, he despatched Pizarro, Alonzo Martin, and some others, to find the nearest way to the sea-shore. This was soon done ; and Alonzo on the beach discovered a couple of canoes far above what seemed the limit of the waters. But the tide gradually crept up to the canoes, and Alonzo, entering one of them, called to his companions to bear witness that he was the first to enter upon the Southern Sea. They returned with their information to Balboa, who immediately marched down to the shore, at the head of eighty of his men. With his sword at his side, and his shield on his arm, he strode into the waters up to his thighs ; and summoned his followers to testify that he touched with his body, and took possession of, this sea for the kings of Castile, and would defend their right to it against all comers. That the natives who dwelt upon its shores should have any claim to it seems never to have occurred as possible to the haughty Spaniard !

With Chiapes our bold and wise adventurer had cemented so strict a friendship that when, with a restless energy * inferior only to that of Cortes, he resolved to explore the gulf now known by the name of San Miguel, Chiapes, though warning him that at that period of the year the navigation was hazardous, accompanied him. Balboa asserted, with ready faith, that God would certainly assist them in the enterprise, inasmuch as great service to Him and large increase of the true faith would result from it, by means of the great treasures which, he said, had to be discovered to enable the kings of Castile to wage war against the infidels. The warning of Chiapes proved correct; Balboa was caught in terrible storms,

---

* Las Casas says of him, that " he could not be quiet even while his bread was being baked."

which threatened the destruction of the expedition ; but he reached the territory of a chief called Tumaco, and was kindly entertained. The chief presented him with two hundred and forty large pearls, and ordered his people to fish for more. This pearl fishery the Spaniards prosecuted with much zest ; after which Balboa set out on his return for Darien, passing through the territories of the caciques whom his policy had rendered friendly and obedient.

He arrived at Darien on the 29th of January, 1514, having been absent for four months, less two days. There he continued to rule with mingled firmness and mildne. s, Pizarro still acting as second in command, for several months. But towards the end of the summer a great expedition arrived from Spain, under the leadership of Pedrarias de Avila, to whom the Court of Spain, ignoring the services of Balboa, had entrusted the government of Darien. He landed with eighteen hundred men, sp'endidly equipped ; and, as Balboa had scarce one-third that number, he refrained from offering any oppositicn. Pedrarias was not a wise man, and as a governor he did nothing that he ought to have done, while what he did he had better have left undone. But our business here is not with his doings or misdoings. At first there was little peace between him and Balboa, but the newly-appointed Bishop of Darien interfered to effect a reconciliation ; and after much discussion it was. agreed that Pedrarias should give his daughter in marriage to Balboa, on her arrival from Spain, and that Balboa should lead an expedition to the Pacific. He began his preparations with indefatigable energy, but past differences arose between him and the jealous Governor, whose suspicions were aroused by some of Balboa's careless utterances. He sent Pizarro to arrest him in the Isle of Tortoises. He was charged with insubordination, disobedience, and treason, found guilty, and beheaded. Such was the unfortunate end of a man second only to Columbus and Cortes among the heroes of American discovery and conquest.

The command of the Pacific expedition was given by Pedrarias to a cousin of his, named Morales; but as he was wholly ignorant of the country and its inhabitants, Pedrarias associated Pizarro with him. The two leaders crossed the isthmus and reached its western shore in safety. Leaving half their force on the mainland, they set out in canoes for a group of islands famous among the Indians for their pearl fishery. The natives offered a vehement opposition as they disembarked on the largest, and there was much hard fighting before the Spaniards effected a lodgment. Their search for pearls was rewarded by a large number, conspicuous for their size and beauty ; they also obtained much gold ; and, loaded with this booty, the whole company returned triumphant to Darien. Pedrarias, when he saw such irrefragable evidence of the affluence of the west coast, and was told of the amenity of its climate and the beauty of its scenery, hastened to remove thither his seat of government ; and, accompanied by Pizarro, he crossed the isthmus, and founded, at the head of a sheltered bay, the famous town of Panama. There Pizarro, who had grown rich in his various expeditions, built himself a house, and bought lands, and maintained a retinue of servants ; for he was a man who delighted in external show and bravery —who loved to surround himself with the pomp and circumstance of wealth. But he bore in his memory the words of the young Indian cacique, and his thoughts constantly turned towards that fair southern land beside the waters of the Pacific where boundless treasures awaited the disposal of the fortunate adve.turer. He longed in his heart to play the first part in some great expedition, and to acquire as world-wide a fame as his kinsman Cortes, the conqueror of Mexico. He felt that he possessed the capacity for command, and that fortune could put before him no opportunity to which he would prove unequal. In the prime of life, with a rich store of experience as a soldier and an explorer, stalwart in body, vigorous in mind, he scorned to think of any enterprise as too difficult for his accomplishment.

While he was indulging his fancy in dreams of a glowing future, the scene of which was always the golden land of the south, there arrived at Panama a sea captain named Andagoya, after a long but not a prosperous voyage in a southward direction. He had to tell of a long extent of coast, covered at intervals by fair green islands ; of a southern range of mountains running parallel to the sea-line, and with snow crowned peaks, shutting out, apparently, the countries that lay beyond ; and of a land abounding in precious metals, of the wealth of which he was informed by all the natives with whom he had opened communications. This exciting narrative

finally determined Pizarro to undertake the conquest of
the rich southern land; but as he was not wealthy
enough to fit out an expedition wholly at his own cost
he made known his designs to one of his associates, a
soldier of fortune like himself, Diego de Almagro. As
Almagro plays an eminent part in the strange drama
we are about to unfold, a word or two may be said in
description of his character. His birth was as obscure
as his comrade's; he had been trained in the hard
experiences of military life, and in a long career of service
had amassed considerable wealth. Frank, generous, and
open-hearted, he was as courageous as Pizarro; but as
a military leader he was inferior to him, and he did not
possess his mastery of the minds of men; he had neither
his fertility of resource, his subtlety of policy, or his
knowledge of the world. The two associates secured the
co-operation of an opulent ecclesiastic, named Hernando
de Luque, the vicar of Panama; a man whose feverish
ambition could not be concealed by his priestly robes,
and who now, in the hope of gratifying his ambition,
agreed to furnish the greater portion of the necessary
expenditure. It was agreed that the booty acquired
should be divided into three equal shares; that Pizarro
should lead the first armament, that Almagro should follow
with supplies and reinforcements, and that De Luque
should remain at Panama to superintend the general interests of the expedition. The approval of Pedrarias, the
Governor, was next obtained; and then the three associates met to consecrate, by the highest act of religious
worship, their contemplated invasion and subjugation of

an unknown and unoffending people. After saying mass, the priest divided the Holy Host into three portions, of which he assumed one himself and administered the others to his companions. It was supposed that the Divine sanction and benediction were thus secured to their daring enterprise, one of the objects of which was, of course, the conversion of the conquered peoples to the Christian Church ; for the humblest and most violent of the Spanish freebooters always looked upon himself as charged with the solemn mission of a propagator of the faith. No doubt it was an ample satisfaction to his conscience, that if he robbed the Indians of their gold, he gave them in place of it a breviary and a rosary; if in one hand he brandished the sword of extermination, in the other he put forward the cross of redemption. The mixed motives which govern human action are always an interesting subject of philosophical analysis ; but surely never was there a stranger combination than in the minds of the Spanish conquerors of the New World ; never was there a combination which would better repay the critical investigator.

On the morning of the 14th of November, 1524, after a solemn celebration of high mass in the cathedral, Pizarro, with the Governor at his side, marched at the head of his men to the sea-shore, followed by nearly the whole population of Panama. Amid a storm of shouts and acclamations, he took leave of Pedrarias, embraced his friends Almagro and Luque, and, with a small company of one hundred and twelve adventurers, embarked on board a couple of small vessels that had been fitted up for his voyage. The wind was fair, and without delay he weighed anchor, shook out his canvas, and firing a farewell from his guns, put out to sea. After a short stay at the Isle of Pearls, he steered to the southward, and, coming to the mouth of a river, sailed up it for about six miles, where he landed. The neighbourhood proved to be dreary and desolate in the extreme—a wide tract of swamp, surrounded by a barren region of desert ; and after some days spent in fruitless exploration, Pizarro was glad to re-embark and continue his voyage. A second landing, further south, yielded no more favourable result, and the dauntless captain sailed onward to the south ; but a great storm arose, and for six or seven days and nights the small and crazy ships, leaking in every seam, were tossed to and fro on the raging waters. It is marvellous that Pizarro, who was no seaman, should have weathered such a gale in safety ; probably the very smallness and lightness of the Spanish vessels contributed to their safety. At last the hurricane subsided, only to expose the adventurers to a new terror. The ships had been provisioned for a very few days, as it was supposed they would be able to pick up fresh supplies along the coast. They had been seriously delayed by the storm ; the provisions had fallen short, and famine stared Pizarro in the face. Each man's rations were reduced to two ears of corn, and Pizarro hastened back to the inlet where he had effected his second disembarkation. Without delay he set to work to repair and refit his ships, while some of his men, now reduced to only eighty in number, started inland in various directions, across swamp and desert, to see if any natives could be found, or supplies of food collected. Every effort failed ; and Pizarro, resolute not to return to Panama unsuccessful, despatched one of his ships, under a faithful adherent named Montenegro, to procure provisions at the Isle of Pearls, while he himself and the larger proportion of the crews endured as best they could the miseries of that desolate shore.

He expected that Montenegro would return within a fortnight; but the third week came, and no Montenegro! The third week passed, and no welcome sail hove in sight; the fourth week glided by,—slowly enough, you may be sure, to men racked with hunger and burning with thirst,—to men exposed to every inclemency of the weather, and weakened by exposure to the malaria of the swamps,—and still the longed-for succour did not arrive. Only the fortitude, the courage, and the moral ascendency of Pizarro enabled his men to sustain the long agony with patience ; but they never upbraided him. They were silent even when they drank the poisonous water that stagnated in the rank morass ; even when they fastened their teeth in the tanned cowhide that coated the ship's pumps ; even when they devoured the acrid berries of the palm and the briny seaweed which the kindly waves cast up on the beach ; for Pizarro's noble example inspired them with a similar heroism of endurance. He ate what they ate, and drank what they drank ; he waited upon the sick, and administered the few medicines he had at his disposal ; he arranged soft beds of leaves and grass for them to lie upon ; he assisted in the erection of huts for their shelter ; he had for every one a cheerful word and a hopeful smile, and that brave earnest look which goes to the heart like an inspiration. One day, while he was thus engaged, two of his men brought him the startling intelligence that, a great way off, they had seen a light moving through the trees. Taking with him twelve armed men, he started at once in the direction indicated, and came upon a cluster of Indian huts, in which he discovered a store of cocoanuts and maize. Who shall tell the joy of the little company when he and his men returned to their wretched settlement laden with such a promise of life?

It was then the forty-seventh day since Montenegro's departure ; happily it witnessed his return. He brought with him a good supply of corn and pork ; and having refreshed themselves with a hearty meal, the whole body prepared to take leave of the Port of Famine (*Puerto de la Hambre*), where they had buried no fewer than twenty-seven of their number. After a short voyage they put into an inlet, which they named *Puerto de la Candaleria*, because it was Candlemas Day (the Feast of the Purification) on which they arrived there. It was no place, however, for a permanent settlement.. Swarms of mosquitoes infested it, and the climate was so damp that it rotted their broad-flapped hats and the linen vests which they wore over their armour. Penetrating into a wood, they came upon a small Indian town ; it was deserted, but they found some ornaments of gold, some maize, and roots, and pork ; also, in vessels at the fire, the significant evidence of cannibalism in human feet and hands. They quickly departed from so uninviting a neighbourhood, and landed next at a place called the *Pueblo Quemado.* Here they discovered an abundance of provisions in another deserted town, which stood upon an eminence, in a position capable of defence. Pizarro was disposed to occupy it until he was reinforced, and able to continue his southward advances, but was foiled by an untoward event. He despatched Gil de Monte-negro on a foray to secure some of the Indians as hostages and guides; but they proved to be of a warlike race, and in a large body attacked the Spaniards, killing two, and wounding several. Their own losses, however, were very considerable, so that they feigned to retreat; and making a swift circuit, suddenly pounced upon Pizarro and the few men who were with him. Pizarro fought like a Paladin. The Indians, perceiving that he was the leader, directed the full force of their assault upon him. He received severe wounds, and was brought to the ground; but speedily recovering himself, he maintained the fight, and, with his men, held his ground until Montenegro arrived, and drove the Indians into swift retreat.

Pizarro had now but one ship at his disposal, and this leaked sorely. Provisions were again running short; his followers were sadly thinned by death and disease, and he recognized the hopelessness of pursuing the expe-dition with such inadequate means. Still, such was his stubborn perseverance, such the tenacity with which he clung to a purpose once resolved upon, that he would not return to Panama, but halted on the way at Chicamá, opposite the Isle of Pearls. It was a sickly, humid

ALTERCATION BETWEEN PIZARRO AND ALMAGRO.

inhospitable spot, where the rains seemed perpetual ; but it answered Pizarro's object, and he disembarked his men, sending on his treasures to Pedrarias, with the golden ornaments he had found, and a narrative of all that had transpired. Rivera, touching at the Isle of Pearls, learned that Almagro had passed with reinforcements, and sent the welcome intelligence to Pizarro. Almagro, meanwhile, had kept along the coast, searching for his associates ; had landed at the Pueblo Quemada, and after a sharp fight had captured the Indian town, and had sailed onward to the river San Juan. But discovering no traces of Pizarro, he had hastened back to the Isle of Pearls. There he was informed of the where abouts of Pizarro, and the two commanders eventually met at Chicamá. Each had a long and stirring chronicle to relate ; but the relation did not sink their spirits, and it was with much alacrity determined that the expedition should not be abandoned, but that Almagro should return to Panama to enlist more volunteers, while Pizarro remained at Chicamá. Only a " terrible perseverance" would have come to such a resolution in the face of all the sufferings the Spaniards had endured ; in face of the melancholy fact that out of a hundred and eighty-two men who had joined the ranks of Pizarro and Almagro respec.ively, one hundred and thirty had perished in the short space of nine months.

Almagro made his way back to Panama, where he met with a most ungracious reception from Pedrarias. De Luque once more exerted his influence, and the Governor was finally persuaded into issuing his licence for the levy of additional recruits; but his indignation against Pizarro, whom he blamed for the loss of life that had taken place, was so great that he insisted on joining Almagro with him in the command. Two ships were bought and fitted out, and with a hundred and ten men, arms, stores, and provisions, Almagro once more set sail from Panama. Having rejoined Pizarro, the two friends steered southward with resolute hearts, and arrived at a river near the San Juan, which they named the Cartagena. There they surprised an Indian town, took some prisoners, and a quantity of gold. But they did not fail to see that their forces were insufficient to carry out the enterprise they had undertaken. There was treasure to be had, and a great country to be colonized, if the men could be got. Again Almagro was sent back to Panama in one of the ships, while Pizarro established himself on the banks of the San Juan. He sent Ruiz, his pilot, with the other vessel, on a cruise to the southward, and in the interval satisfied his restless nature by excursions into the interior. It is a striking proof of the ascendency he had obtained, that his men consented to the labours and underwent the hardships he imposed upon them. In his journeys they penetrated dense and almost impervious forests, traversed dangerous marshes, clambered up rocky banks. They were harassed by incessant clouds of mosquitoes, stung by snakes, attacked by alligators, and wounded by Indian arrows. Hunger they had to endure, and fatigue, and tropical rains. It was a welcome stimulus to their jaded spirits when Ruiz returned with tidings full of promise. He had discovered the Island of Gallo and the Bay of

San Mateo ; and while sailing in a south-westerly direction had fallen in with a kind of raft, or flat-bottomed
boat, propelled by a lateen sail, which had on board
pottery, and finely-wrought woollen cloths, and ornaments
of silver and gold,* besides two young men and three
women, natives of a place called Tumbez. These spoke
to him, apparently by signs, of a king named Huayna
Capac, and of a city of Cuzco, where gold was plentiful.
Ruiz sailed on until, south of the equinoctial line, he
came to a town called Jalongo ; thence he made his way
back to Pizarro, brimming over with stories of a wonderful
region, where the green mountain-sides were dotted with
flocks of sheep (llamas), and the towns were adorned
with palaces and temples, and the districts were traversed
by broad-paved highways of the solidest construction.

Ruiz had not been back many days before Almagro
arrived from Panama, where he had fortunately found
a new Governor installed, Don Pedro de los Rios ; had
enlisted forty new men, and collected a fresh supply of
provisions.† Pizarro and his pale-faced companions

* They had also implements for testing and weighing the precious
metals.

† Oviedo gives an amusing account of the withdrawal of Pedrarias
from his share in the expedition. One day, while he was settling
accounts with the ex-governor, before his *residencia*, or examina ion,
took place, Almagro entered. and said, "Señor, already your lordship knows that in the armada to Peru you are a partner with Captain
Francisco Pizarro, and with the schoolmaster. Don Fernando de
Luque, my companions, and with myself, and that you have not put
anything in it, while we have spent our estates and those of our
friends." And he proceeded to ask him for cattle and money. or
that he would at least pay what was due of his share, and give up

gladly took leave of the mangrove swamps of San Juan, and turned their faces towards the magnetic south. But misfortune still dogged their course; they were assailed by heavy tempests, and compelled to put into the Bay of San Mateo to refit. The question, What shall we do with it? again forced itself upon the consideration of the two commanders. Should they not abandon an enterprise which the very heavens seemed to prohibit? If it were to be prosecuted, must they not obtain more men? Pizarro proposed that this time *he* should return to Panama for reinforcements, and that Almagro should remain,—an offer which led to hot words, and nearly to blows. Both drew their swords; but Rivera, the treasurer, and Ruiz, the pilot, interposed; the friends remembered their ancient friendship, and embraced one another. It was agreed that Almagro should make one more effort at Panama, and that Pizarro should take up his quarters in the island of San Gallo.

There is a striking passage in Sir Walter Raleigh's "History of the World," in which he commends the patient virtue of the Spaniards. "Seldom or never," he

the partnership. Pedrarias angrily replied that Almagro would not so have addressed him had he not been quitting the government, and that had not such been the case, he would have called him and Pizarro to account for the lives that had been lost. Instead of making any payment he demanded four thousand pesos as compensation for surrendering his share in the partnership. Ultimately he consented to take in discharge of his claim one thousand pesos, and an agreement to that effect was signed between him and Almagro; a significant proof of the confidence maintained by the latter, notwithstanding every disaster. in the eventual success of the expedition.— OVIEDO, "Historia Generali," l. 29, c. 23.

says, "do we find that any nation hath endured so many misadventures and miseries as the Spaniards have done in their Indian discoveries; yet, persisting in their enterprises with an invincible constancy, they have annexed to their kingdom so many goodly provinces, as being the remembrance of all dangers past." Of this patient virtue no more splendid example was ever given than that afforded by Pizarro and Almagro; but all Pizarro's soldiers were not of the same mettle, and a certain man called Sarabia was dexterous enough to conceal in a bale of cotton, which Almagro's ship unwittingly conveyed to Panama, a letter to the Governor, setting forth the losses they had sustained, and the sufferings they had endured, and beseeching him to take pity upon them. The petition ended with four lines of doggrel, which obtained a wide circulation in the Indies :—

> " Pues Señor Gobernador,
> Mirelo bien por entero
> Que allá va el Recogedor,
> Y acá queda al Carnicero."*

When this letter fell into the hands of Don Pedro de la Rios he was greatly indignant, forbade the levy of more men for the slaughter-house, and despatched a lawyer named Tafur, with two ships, to fetch from the island of Gallo all who were dissatisfied with the expedition. Not even so crushing a blow as this could break down Pizarro's

Thus freely imitated :—
> " May the lord governor
> Have pity on our woes ;
> For here remains the Butcher, while
> To him the Salesman goes."

E

heroic perseverance.   Addressing his soldiers, he said
that those who wished to return should by all means
do so; but that he was sorry to think that by such a
course they would bring upon themselves harsher sufferings and bitterer want than any they had yet experienced,
and lose that which they had laboured for, just as, in his
belief, they were on the point of discovering something
which would satisfy and enrich them all.   And he
reminded them of the hopeful intelligence they had
obtained from the Indians taken prisoners by Bartolomé
Ruiz.   He concluded by expressing the pleasure he felt
in knowing that whatever they had suffered, he had not
shrunk from being the principal sufferer, preferring always
that he himself should want than that they should; and
so, he said, it always would be.

There was a general cry, however, that they should
depart.   Tafur, who behaved throughout with great impartiality, showed no desire to put any pressure upon
their inclinations; and drawing a line across the vessel's
deck, he took up his station at one end, and placed
Pizarro and his soldiers at the other.   Those, he said,
who were decided on returning to Panama should cross
the line, and come to him; those willing to remain would
stay by Pizarro's side.*   It was found that only fourteen

* The following picturesque verses by an American pen will
probably be new to most of our readers :—

" Pizarro's crimes of perfidy and blood,
   So largely due to training, time. and race,
   Obscure the brilliance of the hero still ;
   Yet once, at least, immortally he stood,
   Sublime in utterance, sublime in will,
   While looking awful Peril in the face,

heroes clung to their veteran commander. Among those were the pilot, Ruiz, and Pedro de Candia.

As soon as Tafur had departed, Pizarro and his four-teen gallant companions removed to the island of Gorgona, which was less open to an attack from the Indians, and there they waited for Almagro, praying

> " He calls his men, and at the leader's word,
> Their presence answers quick, though sore deprest.
> All further ventures would they now resign,
> But lo ! Pizarro traces with his sword
> Along drear Gallo's sand the telling line
> From west to east, and thus his band address :[a] —

> " ' On that side, comrades, toil and hunger wait,
> Battle and death—for some their lives must lose ;
> On this side, truly, safety lies ; but ah !
> On that the glory of a splendid state,
> On this but poverty and Panama.
> Now, as becomes the brave Castilian, choose !

> " ' As for myself, I go towards the south ;
> Let who will follow :' and he passed that bound
> Like Rubicon, enduring, though in sand !
> Spurred by the doughty foot and daring mouth,
> Then followed thirteen of his little band ;
> The die was cast,—at length Peru was found !

> " When powers that serve thee flag. since foiled so long,
> Summon them, soul ! Draw what Pizarro drew ;
> Point to that land of riches, this of lack ;
> Speak as he spake, then cross the line as strong,
> Leaving poor Panama behind thy back,
> To find at last the glory of Peru !"

> *Charlotte Fiske Bates.*

The reader will not fail to note that Miss Bates is not quite accurate in her details. The moral she draws is, however, unaffected by this negligence.

[a] Some authorities represent the division as being made on the sandy shore.

daily,—with that simple piety which lay deep at the hearts of those adventurous men, rough and even cruel as they were,—and subsisting upon shell-fish and seaweed, the refuse of the shore. Patiently enduring the severest hardships, they waited for five months; every morning when they awoke, and every evening before they retired to rest, scanning the horizon with eager eyes in quest of Almagro's vessel. At last a ship hove in sight; she came from Panama, and she brought supplies, but no men; the Governor had refused to allow another enlist-ment,—and we can hardly blame him, when we consider how terrible a fatality had attended the expedition. He had also sent orders for Pizarro and his men to return in six months.

The stern adventurer resolved, nevertheless, on one more struggle with fortune ; and persuading the crew of the Panama ship to join the enterprise, he cheerily steered away to the south-east under full sail, confident that he would yet realize the fruition of his hopes. After touching at several unimportant villages, he landed on a small island, near the mainland, to which he gave the name of Santa Clara. It proved to be a sacred place, to which the inhabitants of the mainland some-times resorted to offer sacrifices. There was a great stone idol, fashioned to resemble a man, but with the head like a cone ; there were also rich gifts of gold and silver, wrought in various shapes, and exquisitely woven mantles, dyed yellow, the mourning colour of the Peruvians. Resuming his voyage, Pizarro met with five rafts, bound on a hostile expedition against the island of

STONE IDOL OF THE PERUVIANS.

Puna; but he bade them accompany him to Tumbez, an important town on the mainland, and sent the men ashore with a message to its rulers. Considerably astonished were they by the appearance of the Spanish vessel, and of the white and bearded men on board; but they determined to show their hospitality to the strangers, and despatched a rich present for them in charge of a personage of distinction whom, from the shape of his ears—an artificial deformity, adopted as a sign of rank— they called an Orejon. Between this Orejon and Pizarro ensued much interesting conversation, and when he went on shore he was accompanied by Alonso de Molina, as Pizarro's representative, and a negro.

If the aspect of a white man had startled the people of Tumbez, they were still more surprised at that of a black man, and made vigorous attempts at that pro- verbially useless operation, washing a blackamoor white. Keen, too, was their astonishment at some animals— two swine, a cock, and a few hens—which the Spaniard brought as a gift; when the cock crew, they asked what it said ! But the surprise and astonishment of the people of Tumbez did not equal the surprise and astonishment with which Alonso de Molina regarded the indications of Peruvian civilization that surrounded him ; and he re- turned to the ship to tell with wonder of the well-built aqueducts, of the stone houses, of a fortress with six or seven walls, of the vessels of silver and gold. To obtain a confirmation of Molina's story, Pizarro sent ashore Pedro de Candia, a tall cavalier of goodly presence, who, clothed in shining armour, with his sword by his side

his shield in his left and a wooden cross in his right
hand, strode through the principal street of Tumbez, the
observed of all observers. I suppose it was as a test of
his courage that the people let loose upon him two wild
animals, apparently a puma and a jaguar. At all events,
he showed no discomposure, and the animals displayed
no inclination to attack him. After this wonderful proof
of the white man's superiority, the natives literally bowed
down before him. They led him in procession to see
the palace and the temple, where gold—gold—gold, on
every side and in every shape, met his enraptured eyes.
The gardens, he observed, were adorned with animals
carved in gold, and flowers and plants beautifully
imitated in the same metal. Before he left, they asked
him to make his gun "speak;" and setting up a board
he fired at it. The loud report, the flash, the smoke,
and the board shivered into fragments, overpowered the
Indians; some, falling on their knees, hid their faces in
their hands; others shrieked; others fled in a panic of
fear. So, in a blaze of glory, the noble Greek took his
departure, and returned on board.

Pizarro was now satisfied that the fulfilment of his
bravest dreams was at hand. He sailed, however, a
little further south, passing Collaque, and reaching
Puerto de Santa, where he met with a cordial reception,
and was entrusted with a couple of Indian youths to go
with him and learn the Castilian language. These boys
were christened Martin and Felipillo. He also obtained
some *llamas* (sheep, the Spaniards called them), vessels
of gold and silver, and various specimens of Indian

taste and ingenuity. Then he crowded on all sail for
Panama, arriving there towards the end of 1527. He
had been absent nearly three years; and, as Robertson
remarks, "no adventurer of the age suffered hardships
or encountered dangers equalling those to which he was
exposed during this long period. The patience with
which he endured the one, and the fortitude with which
he surmounted the other, exceed whatever is recorded in
the history of the New World, where so many romantic
displays of these virtues occur."

At Panama he met with a reception worthy of his
deserts; and the narrative of his expedition excited both
surprise and admiration. But the Governor steadily
refused to sanction another attempt, alleging that the
colony was not strong enough to engage in the conquest
of so mighty an empire as that of Peru. The three
associates, however, were more than ever convinced
that their enterprise was destined to be crowned with
success, and were determined not to be shut out from
the immense fortune that awaited their disposal. They
resolved to appeal for assistance and approval to an
authority much higher than the Governor's; to lay their
petition at the feet of the King himself, the potent
Charles V. For this delicate mission Pizarro was
selected; and it was agreed that he should solicit the
royal permission to equip a new expedition, that he
should obtain for himself the dignity of governor, for
Almagro that of lieutenant-governor, and for Luque the
high office of bishop in the country which they intended
to conquer. So reduced were the resources of the three

friends that it was with difficulty they raised the money to defray the cost of Pizarro's voyage to Europe. Scarcely any fact, perhaps, affords a more striking illustration of the boundless audacity which led them to meditate the conquest of a great and powerful kingdom. It was probably this lack of means which decided them in sending Pizarro alone; for Luque, it is evident, would have preferred that he should have been accompanied by Almagro. "Please God, my children," he exclaimed, "that you do not steal the blessing one from the other, as Jacob did from Esau. I would that you had gone both together."

Pizarro arrived safely in Spain. But his cup of bitterness was not yet full. He had not long been ashore before he was arrested and thrown into prison at the suit of the Bachiller Enciso, in connection, I suppose, with Ojeda's disastrous expedition. By some means or other he speedily obtained his release, and made his way to Seville, where he obtained admission to the presence of the Emperor. His stalwart bearing, his grave deportment, and the natural air of dignity which marked him out as a leader of men, produced a favourable impression; and the impression was deepened by the force and simplicity with which he narrated his sufferings, described his adventures, and indicated his prospects. Charles V. viewed with interest the specimens he had brought with him of Peruvian workmanship, the llamas, and the ornaments of gold, while the courtiers seemed never to weary of contemplating the Indians who had accompanied Pizarro to Spain. Among the visitors to the Imperial Court at this time was Hernando Cortes, the famous conqueror of Mexico. He was a distant relation of Pizarro; admired his dauntless courage and stubborn perseverance, and strongly supported his suit to the Emperor. That suit, was entirely successful. The Emperor, by a formal "capitulation" (as it was called), gave his imperial sanction to the projected expedition against Peru, of which country Pizarro was appointed Governor-General and Adelantado for life, with an ample salary; the extent of his dominions being defined as two hundred leagues down the coast, from Tenumpuela to Chincha. Luque was appointed Bishop of Tumbez, and Almagro commander of the same place; while Ruiz was invested with the sonorous title of Grand Pilot of the Southern Ocean. The heroic men who had remained faithful to Pizarro in the island of Gallo were created *hidalgos*, and Pizarro, as a knight of the Order of Santiago, was admitted to the ranks of chivalry. On his part he agreed to raise two hundred and fifty soldiers at his own expense, and he undertook to set out for Peru within six months from his arrival at Panama.

It is said that a prophet receives no honour in his own country, or from his own kinsmen; but Pizarro, on visiting Trujillo, was warmly received by his brothers, and they entertained so full a confidence in him and his promises that they agreed to sell their estates and embark the result in his enterprise. There were four of them—Hernando (the only legitimate one), Juan, Gonzalo, and Martin; all men of thews and muscles, brave as lions, and prompt of action, while Hernando was almost equal to Francisco himself in mental power and daring. Their united resources, however, were inadequate to the end in view ; and even with some help from Cortes, Pizarro was unable to enlist more than one hundred and twenty-five men ; so that, after obtaining his patents from the Crown, he was compelled to steal out of the port of Seville, in order to elude the scrutiny of the king's officers, who were charged to examine whether he had fulfilled the stipulations of his contract. His little flotilla of three small ships crossed the Atlantic in safety, and in the summer of 1530 arrived at Nombre de Dios, on the side of the isthmus opposite to Panama. Here Almagro and De Luque were waiting to receive him, and learn the result of his mission. Luque was well satisfied, for the bishopric was all he had desired or expected ; but Almagro waxed indignant when he found himself virtually ignored in the distribution of honours. Nor was he well pleased at the arrival of Pizarro's brothers, which he not unnaturally regarded as a circumstance unfavourable to his interests. Pizarro, however, was determined not to risk the ruin of the enterprise by dividing his authority. After much angry discussion, which left its evil effects on the minds of both, it was agreed that Pizarro should give up his office of Adelantado to Almagro, which still left him the sole military and civil authority, and pledge himself not to promote his brothers until Almagro's claims had been fully satisfied.

This difficulty removed, the confederacy was formally

renewed on its original terms, namely, that each associate should share the expenses, and that the profits accruing from it should be equally divided. The preparations were then pushed forward with the utmost alacrity; so that Pizarro was able to set out from Panama on the 28th of December, 1530, in three small ships, carrying one hundred and eighty-three men and thirty-seven horses. He was accompanied by his three stalwart brothers, Ferdinand, Juan, and Gonzalo, and by his maternal uncle, Francisco de Alcantara, a cavalier of dauntless courage and inflexible intrepidity. Almagro was left at Panama, to follow, as soon as possible, with a reinforcement.

One hundred and eighty-three men, of whom thirty-seven were mounted,—such was the force with which Pizarro proposed to conquer a great and wealthy kingdom, which, at the epoch of his invasion, is supposed to have had a population of many millions. But the Spaniards had learned to feel an implicit confidence in their superiority over the American people, and the wonderful successes of Cortes in Mexico had raised this confidence to the highest pitch. It was largely in their favour that Peru was divided and weakened by internal dissensions, while there can be no doubt that its inhabitants were vastly inferior to the Aztecs in all martial qualities.

CHAPTER III.

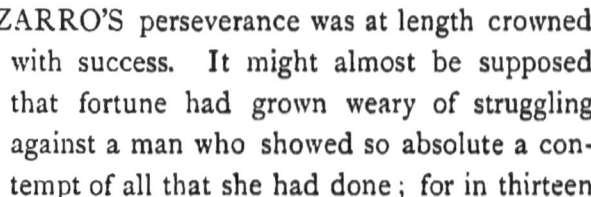

IZARRO'S perseverance was at length crowned with success. It might almost be supposed that fortune had grown weary of struggling against a man who showed so absolute a contempt of all that she had done; for in thirteen days his ships voyaged safely to the Bay of San Mateo, which he had previously been unable to reach in as many months. He immediately landed his little force, and set out on his march southward along the coast, so that he might easily retreat to his ships if too heavily pressed, or receive any reinforcements which might arrive from Panama. Like a true leader, he placed himself in the van, and undauntedly pursued his way over swamp and bog, and across chasm and torrent; never showing any sign of weariness or depression, and inspiring his followers with something of his own heroism. On reaching the town of Coaque he ordered an immediate assault, but the flash of the muskets and the tramp of the horses so affrighted the Indians that they stayed not to meet his charge, but fled headlong into the woods. A rare booty in gold, silver, and emeralds—a kind of foretaste or anticipation of the treasures of Peru—was found at Coaque, greatly inspiriting the adventurers ; and Pizarro hastened to send one of his vessels with a portion of the spoil to Panama, persuaded that it would facilitate the despatch of reinforcements. Another vessel he despatched to Nicaragua, to make a levy among the soldiers of fortune collected in that colony. Then he resumed his march to the south, but as the road lay over a sandy waste, and under a blazing sun, the Spaniards suffered severely. An infectious disease spread through their ranks ; they went to bed well at night, but woke in the morning strangely sick and feeble, and disfigured by horrid ulcers. They also experienced a deficiency of provisions, and as they passed but few villages, and these deserted, they could obtain no fresh supplies. Yet, as Helps remarks, all their miseries were amply repaid by the delay which caused them, as far as regarded the ultimate success of the undertaking. " Each day that Pizarro's men were wasting away by sickness (their losses being told by units), the Peruvians were busy in destroy-ing their thousands, and in sapping the basis of their empire, by a civil warfare, carried to the extreme of barbarous hostility."

About seven months had elapsed since his departure from Panama when Pizarro, one day, descried a ship bearing down upon the coast. He ordered his standard-bearers to hasten along the shore and wave their ban-ners. These were seen by the stranger, which soon afterwards brought-to at an easy distance from the beach, and dropped anchor. To the great joy of the Spaniards she was laden with provisions, and she had on board some officers, despatched by the Emperor, to accompany the expedition. A few days later, when they had marched onwards to the harbour of Puerto Viejo, another ship arrived, bringing thirty foot soldiers, under a veteran named Belalcazar. The reinforcement was small in itself, but it strengthened and confirmed Pizarro's hopes, and he gave the word to march. Some of his soldiers, however, were so charmed by the grateful shades of Puerto Viejo, with its luxuriant vegetation and luscious fruit, with its bland yet refreshing air, with its glorious prospects of a silver-shining ocean if they looked before them, and a grand range of snow-crowned mountain heights if they looked behind them, that they were fain to linger there, and in this Eden of the Pacific coast to found a colony. The desire for repose was natural after the hardships and fatigues they had undergone, but Pizarro was no lotus-eater —a restless activity consumed him. The vision of the Peruvian kingdom was always before his eyes, and in a spirited speech he called on his soldiers to persevere in their great enterprise. Like Tennyson's Ulysses, he felt that he could not "rest from travel," but must drink "life to the lees." We can imagine that he may have used to himself some such words as the poet's hero uses :—

" Souls that have toil'd, and wrought, and thought with me,—
That ever with a frolic welcome took
The thunder and the sunshine, and opposed
Free hearts, free foreheads,— . . .
Death closes all : but something ere the end,
Some work of noble note, may yet be done."

A swift march brought the invaders to the well-known shores of the Bay of Guayaquil, which embraces within its waves the islands of Puna and Santa Clara. On the opposite bend of the bay stood the town of Tumbez, with its domed roofs flashing in the sun. To gain possession of this town was one of Pizarro's principal objects. But while he was meditating an attack, messengers arrived from the cacique of the island of Puna, offering him hospitality. The offer was accepted through the Indian interpreters, whom he had carried to Panama that they might learn Spanish, and who were now attached to his expedition. A number of large *balsas*, or rafts, each pro-pelled by a huge brown sail, conveyed the Spaniards, with their horses and baggage, across the strait that separated the mainland from the green shores of Puna, where a splendid reception awaited them. The natives, who were dressed in cloaks of the gayest colours, and bedizened with golden ornaments, welcomed them with fantastic dances and the sounds of rude musical instruments, enter-tained them to a banquet of fruits and vegetables, and allotted to them as their quarters a green hill-side, stretch-ing down through the forest to the sunny shore. Here Pizarro and his men remained for some time, until it was ascertained through the interpreters that the chiefs of the island were preparing to attack them, though of the cause of so violent a change of sentiment the contemporary historians of the expedition give us no inkling. Pizarro endeavoured to anticipate the attack, and surrounding the chief cacique's house took him and his sons prisoners, and conveyed them to his camp. But by this blow the

F

islanders were rather angered than intimidated, and just before dawn they assailed the Spanish position in great force, raining upon it incessant volleys of darts and arrows.   Pizarro immediately replied with a volley of musketry, and a fierce struggle ensued, which lasted for some hours.   Several Spaniards and some of the horses were wounded, but their superiority was fully established, and from a field strewn with their dead and dying the Indians retreated in great disorder, pursued by the Spanish horsemen.   Profiting by his victory, Pizarro swept the island with fire and sword; plundering the villages, burning the houses, seizing upon any article of value.   He sent to the stake or the scaffold ten of the principal inhabitants, but released the cacique, on the ground that he had taken no share in the outbreak, and to the intent that he might reassemble the scattered and terrified natives in their villages.

Having exhausted the island of all its treasures, Pizarro resolved to proceed to Tumbez.   He sent his baggage across the bay on rafts, each having three armed men on board; he himself, with his soldiers and horses, embarked in three of his own ships.   On arriving at Tumbez he took possession of the town, which he found partly in ruins and deserted; but was surprised to see nothing of his rafts.   Sending out reconnoitring parties, he ascertained that the Indians had seized and broken up his rafts, carried off their cargoes, and killed the Spaniards in charge of them.   He immediately despatched Hernando Pizarro, with eighty foot soldiers and forty cavalry, to pursue and punish the offending Indians.   Hernando crossed a broad deep river on a great raft, overtook the people of Tumbez, and slaughtered them without mercy. Having read this terrible lesson to the unfortunate Indians, the Knight of the Order of Santiago quitted Tumbez on the 18th of May, and resumed his southward march. He had previously been joined by the famous Hernando de Soto with a hundred cavaliers and some horses, and his little army therefore presented quite a formidable aspect. Many of the Indian villages received him hospitably, and these were well treated ; at others, as at Almotuxe and Cacherá, he slew the curacas, or chiefs, and principal inhabitants, in pursuance of his cruel, but not ineffective, policy, of striking terror into the hearts of all opponents.

On arriving at Tangarala he found himself in a fair green valley, through which a shining stream poured its clear waters into the Pacific. Near its mouth, and on a gently-swelling knoll, he resolved to found a colony, and set his men to work to fell timber and collect heavy blocks of stone; after which he traced the boundaries of his new town ; divided the surrounding lands amongst those of his soldiers whom he intended to settle there; apportioned to each of them a certain number of Indians ;* and erected a church, store-houses, and a small fort. To this settlement its founder gave the name of San Miguel (or St. Michael).

Here Pizarro tarried for several months. It is notice-

* A plan "judged to be useful to religion and profitable to the natives, that the new inhabitants might be maintained and the Indians instructed in the faith, conformably to the orders of His Majesty, until it should be decided what was most suitable for the service of God and of the king, and most advantageous to the natives."

able, by the way, that in the conquest of Peru he showed
none of that immense and inexhaustible energy which
Cortes had shown in his conquest of Mexico. He was
tenacious, persevering, patient in the execution of his
designs, but he infused into them no special vigour or
animation. His progress from San Mateo was as leisurely
as that of a king engaged in a calm survey of the resources
of his kingdom ; had in it none of the rapidity and fire
and resistless impetuosity of a conqueror bent on the
acquisition of a mighty territory. This difference between
Pizarro and Cortes was due entirely to a difference of
temper and character ; for the conditions under which
the former invaded Peru were far more favourable than
those under which Cortes invaded Mexico. Cortes had
to be constantly on his guard against the jealous intrigues
of the authorities at Cuba ; had no means of obtaining
continual supplies of arms and provisions ; had no such
depôt to fall back upon as Pizarro had at Panama.
Pizarro, moreover, acted under the direct commission of
Charles V.,—Cortes was without the imperial sanction.
Again, the warriors of Mexico were well armed, well led,
and fought with wonderful resolution and courage ; while
the Peruvians were inefficiently equipped for war, and un-
fitted for it by their irresolute and peaceable disposition.
The conquest of Peru, therefore, remarkable as it was in
many of its features and in its results, was inferior in bold-
ness of design and grandeur of execution to the conquest of
Mexico ; just as Pizarro was inferior in energy, in military
skill, and organizing ability to Cortes. The distinctive
feature of his character was his strenuous perseverance.

However frequently repulsed and beaten, he was always ready to renew his efforts. He worked slowly—he worked with an imperfect idea of what he wanted, but he continued to work. From the first he had determined on the conquest of Peru, and to this object he adhered with a pertinacity of resolution that commands our admiration.

While at San Miguel, Pizarro obtained some insight into the internal affairs of Peru. We have seen that Huayna Capac, the twelfth Inca, left two sons, to one of whom, Huascar, or Guascar, he bequeathed his kingdom of Peru; to the other, Atahuallpa (his offspring by a second wife) his kingdom of Quito. This division of the empire was unacceptable to the Peruvians, and, encouraged by their support, he commanded his half-brother to renounce the throne of Quito. On the other hand, Atahuallpa had gained over the veterans of his father's army, and at their head he marched against Huascar, defeating him in battle and taking him prisoner. For politic reasons the victor spared his brother's life, but he put to death all princes of the royal blood on whom he could lay hands. This civil war was in progress when Pizarro landed in the country, and therefore it was that his progress met with no opposition from its chief authorities. He was allowed to penetrate almost to the centre of the empire before its power was put forth to check his career. And now, as if Fortune had determined upon favouring him as lavishly as she had previously persecuted him sorely, Huascar sent messages to him, soliciting his aid against Atahuallpa, whom he denounced as a rebel and an usurper. The acute mind of Pizarro detected at once the advantages to be gained from this divided state of the kingdom which he had invaded, and he determined, without waiting for Almagro's long: expected reinforcements, to push forward, while intestine discord neutralized the Peruvian power against foreign enemies. By taking part with one or other of the competitors, as circumstance might dictate, he would place himself in a position eventually to crush both.

Leaving a small garrison in San Miguel, he set out, on the 24th of September, at the head of 102 foot soldiers, of whom twenty were armed with cross-bows and three with muskets, and sixty-two horsemen, for Caxamalca, where he understood that Atahuallpa was then residing. When about half way on his march, he was met by envoys from Atahuallpa, who brought him a present and some provisions, and the information that their master had been victorious over his enemies. A courteous reply was returned by the Spanish captain. Continuing his march, and resting every night in the fortified stations erected by the Incas at regular intervals along the great Cuzco road, he crossed the territory of a cacique named Cinto. Thence he diverged to the right, and ascended the mountains by a pass which a handful of men might have defended against an army ; but whether Atahuallpa believed in the peaceful mission of the Spaniards, or confidently relied on his vast numerical superiority, he made no attempt to hold it. On the summit of the pass more messages came from the Inca ; he desired to be apprised of the day of Pizarro's arrival, in order that he might arrange

for the supply of abundant provisions to his troops at the
very stations on their march.   The envoys also repeated
the particulars of Atahuallpa's success in the war against
his brother, and of Huascar having been taken prisoner.
Pizarro answered, that to all ambitious men it happened
as it had happened to Huascar ; not only did they not
attain what they had wickedly aimed at, but they lost
also their own property and persons,—a sententious observation, the applicability of which, as a commentary on
his own career, he did not then foresee.   He proceeded
to say that he knew Atahuallpa to be a great king, but
his own master, the king of Spain, was lord of the whole
world, and his very servants were greater princes than the
Inca of Peru.   This mighty monarch had sent him thither
to bring the people to a knowledge of the true God ;
and, with the few Christians who were his companions, he
had already conquered more potent kings than Atahuallpa.
If the Inca, he added, wished to be his friend, and to
receive him as a friend, well and good : he would assist
him in his wars, and he should be allowed to remain on
his throne, as he, Pizarro, intended to cross the country to
the other sea.   On the other hand, if he wished for war,
Pizarro would wage it against him as he had waged it
against the caciques (or *curacas*) of Puna and Tumbez ;
but he would make war upon none, he would do harm
to none, who did not bring it upon himself.

Pizarro resumed his march, and next day arrived from
Atahuallpa the first messenger, a person of dignity, with
the most cordial assurances from Atahuallpa of friendship
and hospitality.   He undertook to accompany the Spanish

army to Caxamalca. It was on Friday, the 15th of November, at the hour of vespers, that they entered the town, which was built at the foot of a mountain-spur, where the level extended about three miles in breadth. Two rivers flowed through the neighbouring valley; over each was a bridge, conducting to the town. Closê to the entrance was a great square, with houses abutting upon two sides of it. These houses were very spacious, and surrounded by walls of masonry about eighteen feet high. Their roofs were formed of straw and timber. The interior in each case was divided into several blocks, each block consisting of eight chambers, and having its own entrance. In front of the square, facing the plain, rose a fortress of stone ; and above the town, on the hillside, was a larger fortress, with a triple enclosure. It was in the great square that Pizarro posted his troops, while he despatched Hernando de Soto, with twenty horsemen, to inform the Inca of his arrival, and invite him to pay him a visit. Soon after, he sent his brother Hernando with twenty more, to support De Soto if any violence should be attempted.

De Soto was admitted at once to the presence of the Inca, whom he found sitting at the entrance of his tent, surrounded by a number of his chiefs and women. He wore the characteristic Incarial head-dress, "a tassel of wool, which looked silk, of a deep crimson colour (*de color de carmin*), two hands in breadth, set on the head with fringes, which descended to the eyes ; a long fine woollen robe clothed his person, and his wrists and fingers blazed with ornaments of gold." While De Soto, through an interpreter, delivered Pizarro's message, he steadily fixed his eyes upon the ground, and neither moved nor spoke. One of his nobles replied; but at this crisis Hernando Pizarro arrived, and to the Spanish captain's brother Atahuallpa himself condescended to speak. He said that Mayçahilica, a curaca of his, on the banks of the river Turicara (that is, near San Miguel), had sent him word of the evil manner in which the Spaniards had used his curacas, putting them in chains. The same chieftain, he added, had informed him that the Spaniards were indifferent warriors, and that he had killed three of them and a horse. Notwithstanding these things he intended on the morrow to visit the Spanish general, and he would be a friend to him and his soldiers. The blood of Hernando Pizarro kindled to fever-heat at the insult thrown upon the courage of the Spaniards. The people of San Miguel, he exclaimed, were as hens, and one horse was sufficient to subdue their whole country. When the Inca saw them fight he would be able to judge whether they were cowards. His brother, the Governor, he said, was well disposed towards the Inca, and if he were troubled by any enemy the Governor would send at once to conquer him. The Inca replied, that at five days' journey were some troublesome Indians whom he could not subdue, and the Christians might go there and assist his loyal people. The horsemen, answered the vehement Hernando,—the horsemen would suffice for the work, if he set his Indians to hunt out the fugitives. At which speech, as we do at a vaunt of the silliness of which we are convinced, Atahuallpa quietly smiled.

De Soto and Hernando, with their cavaliers, returned to Pizarro, who took up his quarters for the night in the palace of the great square, placing his captain of artillery and a couple of guns in the fortress. He instituted a vigilant watch, as he secretly mistrusted Atahuallpa's friendly professions. Early in the morning, more messengers arrived to say that the Inca would arrive in the evening, and that as the Spaniards had come armed to his royal camp, he should come with arms also. " Let him come as he pleases,"—quoth the Spanish captain.

About midday the Inca removed his camp to within half a mile of Caxamalca, and sent yet another envoy to state that he should come without arms, but with a full retinue, and take up his quarters in a house in the town called " the House of the Serpent." Pizarro then made final preparations for his reception. He knew not whether to expect peace or war, but was resolute not to be taken by surprise. The guns in the fortress were trained to bear upon the Peruvian army encamped in the plain below the town. The foot-soldiers were posted at intervals along the streets leading into the great square. The cavalry, with their horses saddled and bridled, remained on the alert in the palace. Pizarro himself quietly kept to his own apartments, having with him twenty picked cavaliers ; for he was resolved, if the Inca came with treacherous intent, to imitate Cortes in his dealings with Montezuma—to seize his person, and hold him as a hostage. The dusky twilight was deepening and darkening into night, when the captain went round his posts, and addressed his men in frank and soldierly language.

He bade them, since they could not fight in the open field, make strongholds of their hearts. There were no others for their protection, nor any succour but that of God, who helped and defended in the greatest dangers those who were engaged in His service. Let them think nothing of the numbers accumulated before them. Though five hundred Indians might be opposed to one Christian, let them show that courage which brave men on such occasions were wont to show, and God would be on their side. At the moment of attack they were to charge the enemy with vehemence and swiftness, and the cavalry were to be mindful that in the rush their horses did not strike against one another.

Apprehending that Atahuallpa designed to attack them under cover of night, Pizarro sent to hasten his arrival, on the plea that he was waiting to entertain him to supper, and could not sit down until he made his appearance. The Inca then prepared to enter the town in great pomp. In the van were three hundred Indians, attired in tunics of many colours—crossed like chequers —and carrying in their hands huge branches of trees, which they used as brooms to sweep clear their monarch's path. Next came three bodies of minstrels in fantastic costumes, singing the soft Peruvian melodies, and dancing the strangest imaginable measures; who were followed by the warriors of noble birth, with their metal cuirasses and helms of gold and silver reflecting gorgeously the last purple rays of the sunset. Then marched five or six thousand of the main body of the Peruvian army; some wearing tunics of vivid blue, others robes of snowiest white, and bearing maces of copper and silver; others, again, in helmets of skin, that flashed with jewels, and their persons curiously arrayed with gems and gold. Apparently all were unarmed, but in reality they wore concealed beneath their tunics small darts and slings, and bags of stones (*porras pequenas, é hondas, é beloas con piedras*). The Inca himself at length approached; sitting on a throne or litter, adorned with plumes of various colours, and almost covered with plates of gold and silver studded with precious stones, he was borne upon the shoulders of his principal attendants. Behind him came the chief officers of his court, carried in the same manner; and the procession was closed with additional battalions of Peruvian troops.

On reaching the centre of the square, the Inca bade his attendants halt. Immediately Pizarro's chaplain, Father Vincent Valverde, advanced, with a crucifix in one hand and a breviary in the other. As he approached, Atahuallpa inquired of one of those Indians who, from supplying them with provisions, knew something about the Spaniards, who and what he was. The man answered that he was "the captain and guide of talk, the minister of the Supreme God, Pachacamác, and His messenger." Father Vincent, having made an obeisance, addressed to the Peruvian a remarkable discourse; remarkable in itself, and no doubt more remarkable still in the version rendered by the uneducated interpreter. It was divided into two parts; the first theological, the second political. In the first he traced the doctrine of the Creation, the fall of Adam, the origin of sin, the incarnation, sufferings

death, and resurrection of Jesus Christ, the appointment
of St. Peter as Prince of the Apostles, the transmis-
sion of his Apostolic power and his office as Vicar of
God to the Popes, who then, now, and always (he said)
had taken, and continued to take, much pains in preach-
ing and teaching to men the Word of God.   In the
second part he narrated the donation made to the King
of Castile by Pope Alexander VI. of all the regions of
the New World, in order that, having conquered their
inhabitants, and driven out from among them all rebels
and obstinate persons, he might govern them wisely, and
bring them to the knowledge of God, and to the obedience of the Church.   Accordingly the King had sent
forth his captains, who had subdued and converted to
the true religion the great islands and the realm of Mexico,
and had now chosen for his lieutenant and ambassador
Don Francisco Pizarro, that the kingdoms of the Inca
might receive the same benefits which those other lands
had received, and that a perpetual alliance might be
concluded between him and the Majesty of Spain.   This
alliance the Father explained as meaning that Atahuallpa
should acknowledge the supreme jurisdiction of the Pope,
give up idolatry, submit to the King of Castile as his
lawful sovereign, and pay him an annual tribute.   If he
refused he would be harassed with war and fire and
blood (*con guerra, a fuego y á sangre*).   Yea, if with an
obstinate mind he resisted, he might take it as a fact
most certain, that as anciently Pharaoh and all his army
perished in the Red Sea, so would he and all his Indians
be destroyed by the Spanish arms.

At the close of the priest's oration, the Inca uttered a deep *Atac* (Alas!); but, mastering his emotion, he proceeded to reply in dignified and moderate language. He observed that he was lord of the dominions over which he reigned by hereditary succession; that he could not conceive how a foreign priest should presume to dispose of lands that had never belonged to him. He declared that he would not pay tribute to the King of Spain; nor would he abandon his worship of the Sun, the immortal deity whom his ancestors had reverenced, for that of the God of the Spaniards, who was liable to death. The Spaniards, he said, or is represented as saying, had more gods than the Peruvians, who adored only Pachacamác, the Supreme God, with the Sun as his subordinate, and the Moon as the sister of the Sun. He added that, of many of the matters related by the priest* he had never heard before, and he did not now understand their meaning: where had he learned things so extraordinary? "In this book," replied Father Valverde, handing to him his breviary. The book was clasped, and Atahuallpa was unable to open it. The priest stepped forward to do this for him; but the Inca, construing his movement into one of disrespect, struck him on the arm, torn open the book, glanced at some of the pages, and flung it contemptuously on the ground. He then said that he well knew what cruel deeds the

---

* Valverde's harangue, according to Robertson, is evidently a translation or paraphrase of the form, concerted by a junto of Spanish divines and lawyers in 1509, for explaining the claim of their king to the sovereignty of the New World.

Spaniards had committed on their march; how they had ill-treated his chiefs, and pillaged his storehouses. Valverde replied that it was some Indians who had been guilty of those offences, and that Pizarro had ordered them to be punished, and was willing to make restitution. "I will stay here," rejoined the Inca, "until you restore to me all that you have taken from my land."

The Father returned to the Governor, and informed him of all that had occurred, giving it as his opinion that further delay was unsafe, and implying that the sword must be called in to effect a settlement. It is probable that up to this moment Pizarro had thought of the capture of the king as an expedient which in certain circumstances might be forced upon him, but had hardly made up his mind to adopt it. The priest's words turned the balance. Putting on a thick cotton tunic as a defence, and taking his sword and buckler, he sent word to his brother Hernando that the moment had come; the latter signalled to the captain of artillery; and amid the roar of cannon and the blaze of trumpets, the Spanish horse-men rushed to the charge. Pizarro made straight for the Inca's litter, followed by his chosen band of cavaliers; but such was the impetuosity of his onset, that only four were close up to him when, cutting his way through the Peruvian body-guard, he seized the unfortunate Atahuallpa by the left arm, shouting the famous war-cry, "Santiago!" With deadly swords his comrades slew the bearers of the litter, which fell to the ground, and immediately the person of the Inca was secured; his robe, in the *mêlee*, being torn to pieces, and his diadem rent in twain.   The Peruvians were so taken by surprise, that they had neither the opportunity nor the presence of mind to make use of their weapons.   Terrified by the tramping and snorting of the horses, they ran hither and thither in wild confusion, and were slaughtered without resistance.   If they rushed frantically to the gates of the square, they found them guarded by companies of Spaniards, who fired upon them, killing and wounding, and drove them back upon the panic-stricken crowd, to perish like sheep in a slaughter-house.   The carnage lasted until nightfall, when the darkness like a shroud descended upon upwards of two thousand dead.[*]

Not a Spaniard was wounded, except Pizarro, who in the scuffle around the Inca's litter received a slight injury in the hand.   Three thousand Peruvians were made prisoners.

After the massacre was over, Pizarro caused the Inca to be re-clothed according to his rank, and endeavoured to comfort him by the assurance that he had fallen into merciful hands, and that he had no need to feel ashamed of having been conquered by one who, like himself, had done great deeds.   The misfortunes that had befallen him and his people were of his own seeking, inasmuch as he had come with a large army, and had treated with scorn the Word of God.   Therefore, the Lord had permitted his pride to be humbled, and had taken care that no Christian should be wounded by an Indian.

---

[*] This is the number given by Pizarro's secretary and biographer, Xeres ; but Garcilasso de la Vega raises it to a total of five thousand, and Sancho to seven thousand.

Atahuallpa, it is said, replied that he had been deceived by his captains, who had told him not to fear the Spaniards, but to go boldly forward with his army and attack them. He had wished to come in the guise of peace, but they had prevented him.

On receiving the reports of his lieutenants, all testifying to the completeness of his success, and to the fact that none of the Spaniards had been killed or wounded, Pizarro gave thanks to God, saying, that so great a victory must be regarded as a miracle due to His favour. He then ordered his troops to retire to their quarters, but that a strict watch should be maintained.

At supper the conqueror and the conquered sat at the same table. Atahuallpa's couch was placed in Pizarro's chamber; he was not subjected to the indignity of bonds, nor was any other guard posted than that which usually attended upon the governor. As soon as morning came, a squadron of thirty horsemen was despatched to recon-noitre, and to plunder the Inca's camp; from which congenial occupation they returned laden with go'd, silver, emeralds, and provisions. The gold alone, when melted, yielded no less a sum than 80,000 pesos. They told P.zarro that they had observed among the dead some who had not fallen beneath Spanish weapons, and Atahuallpa acknowledged that these had been put to death by his orders, because they had been frightened by De Soto's horse. For when that gallant cavalier went on his errand to the Inca, he had thought fit to display the excellent qualities of his famous white charger. At his bidding it had reared and bounded, had wheeled

G

and curvetted, had dashed across the field like a flash
of lightning, and suddenly halted so near the Inca, that
the foam from its mouth had sprinkled his royal robe.
He himself, like a true king, had shown no sign of
astonishment or alarm; but there were many who fled
in terror before a monster of which they had hitherto
had no knowledge. Poor wretches! they were cruelly
punished for their not unnatural cowardice. Their punishment, however, did not reassure their countrymen, who
to the last were greatly affrighted by the Spanish horses,
which played in the conquest of Peru almost as important
a part as their riders.

The disposal of his numerous prisoners was a matter
of great anxiety to Pizarro. He shrank from the ghastly
proposal of some of his officers, that the fighting men
among them should be slaughtered in cold blood. He
was cruel from policy rather than from inclination.
Eventually he gave his soldiers leave to select such
prisoners as they chose to act as their servants; the rest
he set at liberty. In like manner, of the large number
of sheep brought in, those not killed were allowed to
wander away among the mountains. Having despatched
messengers to Panama with the tidings of his victory, he
employed his soldiers in strengthening the fortifications
of Caxamalca, and in erecting a church, being unwilling
to advance into the interior until the long-expected reinforcements arrived. Meanwhile he taught Atahuallpa
to play at chess and at cards, in order that the hours of
his captivity might prove less irksome. The Inca, a
man of quick intelligence, soon learned to speak Spanish,

and showed a vigorous industry in endeavouring to read and write it. Much perplexed to know whether the Spaniards acquired a knowledge of their language by natural instinct, or by toil and pains as he did, he one day asked one of his guards to write the word " God" on his thumb-nail; and when the soldier had done as he wished, he went round among the other soldiers and asked them to read it. Great was his surprise to find that all of them read alike. Pizarro at this moment came upon the scene; whereupon the Inca held up to him his thumb, and begged him to read what was written on it. With a blush, it is said, Pizarro was forced to own that he could not. Thenceforth the Inca, we are told, regarded him with considerably diminished awe and respect.

Such is the common story; but it seems to us very apocryphal. In the first place, that every common soldier should be able to read must be accepted as an almost marvellous occurrence; in the second, it is surely improbable that a man of Pizarro's ability, in the position in which he was placed, should not have mastered that one Spanish word necessarily in common use, and dear to every devout Spaniard. Thirdly, there can be no just reason for supposing that Atahuallpa would attach any special importance to a knowledge of reading and writing, or that Pizarro's deficiency in this respect would lessen his respect for the master of the Spanish battalions, the general who wielded at his will those terrible horsemen and fatal guns. Atahuallpa was a king, not a school-master, and would judge Pizarro by his material power, and not by his possession of the "elements of education."

In the conversations that occurred between the Spanish captain and his prisoner, Pizarro gained a large amount of information respecting the internal condition of Peru. He learned that Atahuallpa's army had captured the great city of Cuzco, and taken prisoner his half-brother and rival, Huascar; he was soon afterwards apprised that the latter had been put to death, and that thus Atahuallpa was sole lord of both Peru and Quito. On his part, he informed the Inca that all the Peruvian territories, and the rest of the New World, belonged, by right of the Papal donation, to the Emperor, Charles V., whom he must thenceforth acknowledge as his superior. This Atahuallpa readily promised ; and having observed the Christian greed of gold, he added, that if he would set him free, he would fill the room in which the two were conversing, up to a mark which he made on the wall, with gold,—vases, and jars, and bars of gold, piled nine feet high.* And this ransom he undertook to collect in two months' time. Pizarro eagerly accepted the splendid proposal, and a line at the stipulated height was drawn all round the room, which measured twenty-two feet in length by sixteen feet in breadth.

Atahuallpa, longing for liberty, and perhaps for revenge, sent in all haste to Cuzco, and Quito, and other places, where gold had been accumulated in large quantities for the decoration of the houses of the gods or the palaces of the Incas, with instructions to his officials to remit

* The height was half as much again as a man's ordinary stature.

what was necessary for making up his ransom to Caxamalca. And such was the loyal obedience of the
Peruvians, that though their sovereign was a prisoner,
they executed his orders with the utmost alacrity.* It
may be assumed that it was their hope of releasing him
by this means, which prevented the Peruvians from
attempting any other method, which would probably
have endangered his life; hence, though the military
force of the empire was still unbroken, no preparations
were made, no army was assembled, to crush the invaders,
and avenge the massacre of Caxamalca. Pizarro's little
army remained unmolested. The opportunity soon
passed; for Almagro, in the middle of December, landed
at Concibi, near Coaque, with a large reinforcement.
About the same time three caravels, with volunteers on
board, arrived from Nicaragua; so that, in all, 160
Spaniards, with 84 horses, were preparing to join the
conquerors at Caxamalca.

Pizarro then felt strong enough to despatch his brother
Hernando to collect the remainder of the ransom, and
to observe the movements of the Peruvian troops. He
took with him some arquebusiers and twenty horsemen.
Wherever he went, his march lay through a rich and
fertile country, whose inhabitants appeared contented
and prosperous; the signs were numerous of a peaceful
and advanced civilization. Along the great paved causeway, which might well be termed one of the wonders of

---

* The reader will be reminded of the efforts of the people of
England to ransom Richard I. from the hands of the German
Emperor.

the world—the famous road which for upwards of a
thousand miles crossed the summit of the Sierras, bridg-
ing chasms and rivers, ascending precipices, descending
rugged declivities—he rode towards Pachacamác. At every
village he was received with dances and merry-makings ;
at all the stations he was freely supplied with llamas,
maize, firewood, and a stimulating drink called *chica.* He
observed that the Peruvians were a religious people,
strict in the performance of the rites and ceremonies
of their Sun-worship; but while most of their temples
were dedicated to the Sun, others were reserved for
" Cuzco the Ancient, father of Atabaliva." In the houses
of the Sun virgins ministered, the altars being stained
with the blood of llamas, and libations of *chica* poured
upon the earth.

Through a populous and fertile country Hernando
descended to Pachacamác, where, as at every point of
his route, he was greeted with a friendly welcome. He
found it to be a large and well-peopled town on the sea-
shore, much of the importance of which was owing to
the fame of its ancient temple. To this temple such
reverence attached, that the Indians spoke of it with
bated breath, and very reluctantly. The whole of the
country round about contributed to its support. It was
of ample dimensions, with large courts and extensive
precincts, but dim and squalid. In a great court outside
the temple were the houses of the virgins. No votary
was admitted into the first inner court unless he had
prepared himself by a twenty days' fast; nor into the
second until he had fasted for a year. There it was

that the chief priest, in a sitting posture, and with his head covered, received the disciples who had completed this prolonged initiation. To him they declared their desires or necessities; and the subordinate ministers, or "Pages of God," retired to an inner chamber to commune with the divinity, who expressed to them his anger or satisfaction, and through them gave orders for offerings and sacrifices. " I believe," says Hernando Pizarro, "that they do not talk with the Devil, but that these ministers of the chief priest deceive the caciques, and this I endeavoured to find out. It happened that one of them, so a cacique told me, had said that he was told by the Devil that the caciques ought not to be afraid of our horses, which might frighten, but could do no harm. I put this man to the torture, but he clung so fiercely to his evil creed, that nothing more could be wrung from him than that he really believed the idol to be a god."

To convince the caciques of the deception under which they grovelled, he strode boldly into the sacred recesses of the temple, tore down the idol from its place of honour, and shattered it in pieces. It is probable, however, that this act of iconoclasm had far less effect on the minds of the Peruvians than the terror of the Spanish arms. We do not desert our gods because they are broken by the hands of others It i only when they abandon us that we are convinced of their feeb'eness and folly.

To the great disappointment of the Spaniards, the priests had removed and concealed the treasures of Pach-acamác on hearing of their approach; and learning that the chief Peruvian general, Chilicuchima, was encamped near

Xauxa with a large army, Hernando marched in that direction. Every mile that he advanced filled him with greater wonderment at the prosperity of the country, where want and poverty seemed utterly unknown, and gold and silver were as plentiful as in fairy tales. In crossing the mountains some of his horses lost their shoes, and as no iron was to be found, Hernando caused them to be re-shod with silver. On his arrival at Xauxa, a large and prosperous town, he entered into communication with Chilicuchima, and easily persuaded him to return with him to Caxamalca, to pay his respects to his captive sovereign. After a successful expedition, in which, strange to say, no blood had been shed, Hernando rode again into Caxamalca, on the 25th of March, 1533, accompanied by the Peruvian general, and bringing with him twenty-seven loads of gold and two thousand marks of silver.

Chilicuchima is described as a robust old man, of soldierly aspect, tall, and with long white hair. His mode of approaching his sovereign indicated the profoundest reverence. At the palace gate he uncovered his head, took off his shoes, and placed a burden on his shoulders. The caciques who attended him did the same. Entering the royal presence, he raised his hands to the sun, and gave thanks that he had been permitted the happiness of seeing his sovereign again. With the tears streaming down his furrowed cheeks he prostrated himself on the ground, and kissed his face, his hands, his feet. The Inca preserved an impassive demeanour, though it is said that he cherished a profound regard for his great captain. He addressed him calmly, as befitted a descendant of the

CHILICUCHIMA.

Sun, and, after a brief interview, dismissed him with a haughty wave of the hand.

During Hernando Pizarro's absence at Pachacamác and Xauxa, his brother despatched three cavaliers to Cuzco, to receive its contribution to the promised ransom, and report upon the appearance and condition of the country. The three chosen were Pedro Moguer, Francisco de Zarate, and Martin Bueno. Escorted by the Inca's brother, and conveyed in luxurious litters, they travelled the whole distance of six hundred miles, through a country which astonished them by its multiplied evidences of prosperity. On their arrival at Cuzco they were welcomed with feasts and dances and songs, and splendidly lodged in a magnificent palace. These unaccustomed honours proved too much for the self-restraint of the Spanish soldiers, and they behaved with so much incontinency, indiscreetness, and grossness—I borrow the words from a Spanish writer—as effectually to disabuse the Indians of their first simple belief that they were the sons of the gods (*hijos de Dios*), and to impress them with the idea that they were a new scourge sent from heaven in punishment of their sins. At one time the Cuzcans contemplated killing them, but forbore out of their dread of Atahuallpa's vengeance, or their fears for his safety, and made haste to free themselves from the humiliation of their presence by conceding all that they demanded. The defect of Pizarro as a statesman is shown in his selection of messengers so unfit for the task committed to them. Cortes would have converted such a mission into a means of conciliating and attaching the Peruvian people, and would have been careful that his envoys should be men worthy of representing the Spanish nation, and capable of advancing its interests.*

The three soldiers returned to Caxamalca with glowing tales of the wonders they had seen. They spoke of Cuzco as if it had been a city of gold, an earthly paradise, that "Dorado" which had figured in the old legends and romances. They declared that the walls of the Temple of the Sun shone resplendent with vast plates of gold, of which they themselves had carried off no fewer than seven hundred; and that it was adorned with an image of the orb of day, all wrought in gold, with rays of gold, which it dazzled the eyes to look upon.

On the 14th of April, during their absence at Cuzco, Almagro and his reinforcements marched into Caxa-

---

* "We may well pause to consider the sufferings of the inhabitants of Cuzco,.as having something peculiar in them, even for the Indies. Their city, in their eyes a Paris, a Rome, and a Jerusalem, was fondly, devotedly, adoringly regarded by them. At any caravanserai, the traveller who was journeying from Cuzco took the precedence— belonging to a superior fortune—of the Peruvian who was only approaching the sacred city. But now Cuzco was desolate and cast down, for in a few brief weeks it had suffered the two greatest evils known in the life of cities. It had recently been occupied by a conquering army of its own people, and had experienced all that the bitterest civil discord let loose in a town can inflict upon it. Hardly had this storm swept over the devoted city, when it was to encounter the frigid insolence of alien victors, who knew nothing of its manners, its religion, or its laws. Was it for this that, by incredible labour' the stones had been adjusted in its palaces so as to appear like the cleavage of the natural rock ? Was it for this that its Temple of the Sun towered conspicuous above all other temples, merely to attract upon it the lightning of destruction from all sides?"—*Sir Arthur Helps*, "Spanish Conquest in America," vol. iii., pp. 561-62.

malca. However agreeable this arrival might be to the Spaniards, it was alarming to the Inca, who saw the power of his enemies largely increased; and as he knew neither the source whence they derived their supplies, nor the means by which they were conveyed to Peru, he could not foresee (says Robertson) to what a height the inundation that poured in upon his dominions might attain. As a matter of fact, had the Inca been a man of any political sagacity, he would have seen in the arrival of Almagro the fulcrum on which to rest a successful effort for the deliverance of his country. He would have detected the rising jealousy between the two Spanish leaders, and availed himself of it to further his own purposes. Nothing, however, is more remarkable in the history of the conquest of the New World than the fact that two great, opulent, and civilized nations fell before a handful of invaders, without producing a single man capable of initiating and conducting a vigorous defence, of stimulating his countrymen to a patriotic resistance.

Almagro, since Pizarro's return from Spain, had suspected him of an intention to arrogate to himself an undue share both of power and plunder. That Pizarro cared much for plunder I do not believe; but a marked feature of his character was his love of power, and that he intended to keep the government of the empire in his own hands cannot be doubted. The time had not come, however, when he could afford to quarrel with his colleague ; and on his arrival at Caxamalca he received him with every demonstration of sincere respect and cordiality, and lodged him in the best quarters. Moreover, as his brother

Hernando, a cavalier of good blood and fine manners, was not slow in exhibiting his scorn of the rough unlettered adventurer, Pizarro resolved to send him on a mission to Spain, in order to prevent any premature disruption of the confederacy. He prepared, therefore, for a division of the treasure which had been collected for Atahuallpa's ransom, that the King's fifth might be ascertained and conveyed to Seville by Hernando. Gold had been accumulated in such shapes and quantities as the most vivid imagination had failed to conceive in its least sober dreams. Goblets of gold, vases of gold, slabs and basins and plates of gold, utensils of gold, rings and bracelets of gold, panels of gold wrenched from the walls of the temple, heavy golden bars which had formed their cornices, fountains of gold, and birds, fruits, and vegetables of gold,—gold everywhere; much of it exquisitely wrought, all without alloy :—

"Gold! fine gold! both yellow and red ;
Beaten and molten, polished and red."

All this mass was melted down into square ingots or bars, and then weighed. It was found to represent in value 1,326,539 pesos ;* or, as money is now valued, about £3.500,000.+ A fifth having been set apart for the king, Pizarro received the next great share (57,222 pesos), along with the massive throne of gold on which Atahuallpa had been brought to Caxamalca; his brother Hernando (with 31,080 pesos), De Soto (with 17,740

* A peso was worth about 4s. 8½d. ; or, at the present value of money, about five times that sum.
† There was also silver to the value of 51,610 marks.

pesos), and the other principal cavaliers came next in the distribution. Then each horse-soldier received 8,880 pesos; and each foot-soldier between 3.000 and 4,000. To Almagro,* in recognition of his share in the enterprise, 100,000 pesos were allotted; and 20.000 pesos were divided among his soldiers, who had borne nothing of the heat and burden of the day. A sum of 2,220 pesos was set apart for the new Christian church of San Francisco, at Caximalca; and 15,000 pesos for the colony of San Miguel† (July 25th).

" There is no example in history," says Robertson,‡ " of such a sudden acquisition of wealth by military service, nor was ever a sum so great divided among so small a number of soldiers. Many of them, having received a recompense for their services far beyond their most sanguine hopes, were so impatient to retire from ⁄fatigue and danger, in order to spend the remainder of their days in ease and opulence, that they demanded their discharge with clamorous importunity. Pizarro,

* Luque had died at Panama a short time before Almagro's departure.

† As is always the case, this vast increase of individual wealth was attended by a great increase in the price of the articles in general demand. A horse could not be bought for less than 1,500 pesos; a sheet of paper cost 10 pesos; a bottle of wine, 70 pesos; even a head of garlic (a condiment almost indispensable to the Spaniard). half a peso. It is recorded by Oviedo as one of the results. and certainly the most curious, of the shower of gold which had descended on the Spaniards, that instead of debtors avoiding their creditors the reverse prevailed, and creditors hid themselves in order to evade payment ! Such a state of things has never obtained in *our* day.

‡ Robertson, " Conquest of America," vol. ii., p. 310. *See* Garcilasso de la Vega. pt. 2. lib. i., c. 38.

sensible that from such men he could not expect enterprise in action nor fortitude in suffering, and persuaded that wherever they went the display of their riches would allure adventurers, less opulent but more hardy, to his standard, granted their suit without reluctance, and permitted above sixty of them to accompany his brother Hernando." Yet as these were veterans, and accustomed to serve under his standard, he must have regretted their departure, which weakened materially his force in comparison with that enlisted by Almagro; and his ready compliance with their demand is one of those instances of generosity which brighten his stormy career.

CHAPTER IV.

DEATH OF ATAHUALLPA.—THE SPANISH SETTLE-
MENT.

AVING paid a magnificent and right royal ransom, Atahuallpa naturally demanded to be set at liberty.* I have no doubt that this was the original intention of Pizarro ; that he would have released him under such con-ditions as would have ensured his subordination to the Spaniards ; but the arrival of Almagro and his men brought about a complete change of affairs. From the

---

* Atahuallpa was well treated in his captivity. He was attended by his wives and concubines, who waited on him at table, and dis-charged the various duties about his person. Indian nobles were stationed in his ante-chamber, though they never entered his pre-sence, unless summoned. His table was served with gold and silver plate. His dress, which he changed frequently, was a robe made of the skins of bats, or a mantle of the finely-woven wool of the *vicuña.* Upon his head• he wore the *llautre,* a woollen turban of the most vivid colours, and round his forehead was twisted the emblematic *borla.* He was taught to play with dice, and in the game of chess he became very expert. In truth, he wanted nothing but that which the captive wants most of all— freedom.—*See* Pedro Pizarro's graphic narrative, App., Prescott, ii , 458, 459.

first they were inimical to the Inca, partly, perhaps, from
a jealous feeling that he should have been captured by
Pizarro and his soldiers ; partly because they feared that
whatever gold might come in would still be claimed as a
portion of his ransom.   This unfavourableness of sentiment was early detected by Atahuallpa, who, when
Hernando Pizarro took leave of him, exclaimed, " I am
sorry that you are going ; for when you are gone, I know
the fat man and the one-eyed man "—that is Riquelma,
the King's treasurer, and Almagro—" will combine to
kill me." He had another and even more powerful
enemy in the interpreter Felipillo, who, to the intense
wrath and shame of the Inca, had presumed to fall in
love with one of his concubines,—an offence against
the monarch's dignity which he felt very keenly. Thus
it came to pass that the question of the disposal of
Atahuallpa was much discussed in the camp, under
influences which did not bode him well. About the
same time rumours reached Pizarro of the gathering of
the Peruvian army, as if it had suddenly awakened from
its long lethargy, and designed to strike a blow for the
national independence. Brave as the Spanish captain
was, and conscious of the superiority he derived from the
arms and discipline of his men, he knew that they were
but a handful in the midst of millions, and that at any
time a well-conceived combination or a skilful surprise
might set aside the superiority on which he relied, and
overwhelm him with ruin. He could not afford, therefore, to throw away a single chance, and the release of
Atahuallpa might have been such a chance, as it would

have afforded the Peruvians a centre, a rallying-point, so to speak, and a legitimate and, in their belief, Heaven-sent leader. On the other hand, if he held him prisoner, he was liable to a thousand annoyances and anxieties; Atahuallpa would naturally intrigue for his liberation or to effect his escape, or the Peruvians would be incited to some desperate attempt on behalf of their imprisoned monarch. Pizarro was perplexed and uneasy; for throughout his Peruvian expedition he was a close copyist of Cortes, and here was a dilemma in which he had no example of Cortes to guide him. In adopting the principle that whatever was expedient was just ("Y esto tenia per justo, pues era provechoso"), he adopted one which Cortes was not fond of recognizing.

His hesitation is shown by the circumstance that he published a formal and official document, fully discharging the Inca of further obligation in respect to the ransom, though its exact terms had not been, and perhaps never would have been, fulfilled. Yet, at the same time, he expressed an opinion that considerations of safety and security rendered necessary the detention of the Inca until additional reinforcements came from Spain. While he thus wavered, the rumours of an Indian attack revived; an army, it was said, was assembling at Quito, and would be supported by 30,000 Caribs; and many tongues connected with this menacing movement the name of Atahuallpa. When Pizarro repeated the story to Chilicuchima, the grey-haired veteran pronounced it a calumny. Pizarro next went to the Inca himself: "What treason is it you are meditating against me? against *me*,

H

who have treated you with honour, and trusted in your
words as in those of a brother?" "Why do you mock
me?" replied the Inca; "why are you always saying these
jests of me? What are we, I and my people,—how can
we conquer men so valiant as yours? Do not cast
these gibes at me." This he said (we are told) with great
composure, but he did not convince Pizarro, who remembered that he had often spoken with the same
coolness and astuteness, so that the Spaniards had been
surprised to see such prudence in a barbarian ("en vu
hombre barbaro tanta prudencia").

Perceiving that he had not removed the general's
suspicions, Atahuallpa again asserted his innocence.
"Am I not," he said, "a captive in your hands?
How could I conceive such a design as you speak of,
when I should be the first victim? And little do you
know of my people if you think they would enter upon
it without my orders, when the very birds in my dominions would not dare to fly in opposition to my will."

But the belief of the troops in a general rising of the
natives deepened every hour. A large force, it was said,
had been concentrated at Guamachucho, some ninety
miles from the camp. . Pizarro seems to have shared
their apprehensions. He caused the Inca to be loaded
with fetters; he doubled his patrols, and went the rounds
in person to see that vigilant watch was kept. The
soldiers slept on their arms; the horses were all saddled
and bridled in readiness for immediate service. What
was more to the purpose, two Indian spies were sent
out to reconnoitre the enemy's position. They returned

with the information that the Peruvian army was slowly
advancing through a mountainous district; that Atahuallpa had at first ordered it to retreat, but had afterwards
cancelled the order, and named the hour and place at
which the attack was to be delivered, saying that if it
were delayed he should be put to death.   The soldiers,
and especially those of Almagro's party, were more
clamorous than ever, and openly declared that Atahuallpa's death was essential to the safety of the Spaniards.
They were supported by Riquelma the treasurer, and
other royal officers, who had accompanied Almagro to
the camp. Pizarro still shrank from so extreme a measure
as the death of his prisoner, and Hernando de Soto and
a few others nobly protested against it, asserting that
there was not sufficient evidence of his guilt.   It occurred
to Pizarro to despatch Soto at the head of a small force
to reconnoitre the country about Guamachucho, and
ascertain if the rumours of warlike movements were
based on fact or fictitious.   But while Soto was absent
there came to the camp at Caxamalca a couple of
Indians, who were attached to the Spanish army, and
they declared that the Peruvians were only three leagues
from Caxamalca, and would attack on that or the
following night. The excitement then became so intense
that Pizarro consented to bring the Inca to immediate
trial.   The usual formalities were observed.   Pizarro
and Almagro presided as judges ; a doctor of laws acted
for the prosecution ; and an advocate was assigned to
the prisoner.   Twelve charges, drawn up in the form of
interrogatories, were preferred. Of these the most impor-

tant were, that the Inca had ordered the assassination
of his brother, and fomented a conspiracy against the
Spaniards. He was also accused of idolatrous and
adulterous practices, and of lavishly and unprofitably
expending the revenues of the kingdom since the conquest, of prosecuting unjust wars, and wasting his estates
upon his kinsmen. It can hardly be said that any of
these matters came within the cognizance of an invading
power, except the alleged conspiracy; but they seem to
have been formally investigated. The principal witnesses were the two Indians, whose evidence was wholly
unsupported; the judges, however, declared Atahuallpa
guilty, and sentenced him to be burnt at the stake. He
was offered another form of death if he embraced Christianity—a religion which could hardly have been recommended to him by the conduct of its Spanish professors !

An angry discussion followed the declaration of the
sentence. Many of the Spaniards protested against its
being carried out. They were not insensible to the claims
of honour, justice, and good faith, and insisted that
Pizarro was bound by the promise he had given. They
even suggested that the Inca should be transferred to
Spain, where the charges against him could be examined
by the proper tribunals. They denied the authority of
the court that had condemned him, and impugned the
validity of the evidence brought before it. In all this
they were fully justified ; the trial was a gross outrage on
the law of nations ; their sole error lay in supposing that
any Spanish tribunal had a right to sit in judgment on
an independent prince. Their courageous and manly

protest failed, however, against the bloodthirstiness and panic fears of the majority,* and all that remained for them was to record in writing their sense of the iniquity of a procedure which has left an indelible blot on the Spanish name.

We acknowledge much force, however, in the reasoning of the historian that this vehement debate, and the large majority against Atahuallpa, militate against the common belief, that his death was the result of a previous and stern resolve on the part of the Spanish commander. I am convinced that Pizarro shared in what was obviously the opinion of most of his soldiers, that the Inca had secretly ordered military preparations, and that he regarded his death as an urgent measure of self-preservation. It must be admitted that this argument does not absolve him from the guilt attaching to so cruel and unprecedented an outrage, but it furnishes an excuse which will be accepted by persons capable of calmly considering the position of the Spaniards, and the hopes and fears by which they were swayed. The whole transaction is an illustration of the great truth which common experience is continually demonstrating, that one ill deed inevitably leads to another, that good cannot come out of evil. The invasion of Peru was the initial crime, and it necessitated a long series of crimes over the record of which our shocked humanity may well turn pale.

When the sentence was communicated to the Inca his emotion was uncontrollable. With tears in his eyes,

---

* The majority numbered 350 ; the minority, 50.

he exclaimed : "What have I or my children done
that I should meet such a fate?" Turning to Pizarro,
he continued, reproachfully: "And from *your* hands!
You, who have received so much kindness and friendship from my people—you, with whom I have shared
my troubles—you, whom I have loaded with benefits!"
He implored him to spare his life, promising double the
ransom already paid, if only time were given him to collect
it, and offering any guarantee that might be required for
the safety of the Spanish army, down to the meanest
soldier. Pizarro listened to this touching appeal with
tears. "I myself," says an eyewitness, "saw the general
weep." But though he wept, he did not—perhaps he
could not—relent; and when Atahuallpa found that
death was inevitable, he prepared to meet it with a
dignity worthy of his rank and race.

By sound of trumpet the Inca's doom was proclaimed
in the great square of Caxamalca; and two hours after
sunset, on the 29th of August, it was carried into execution. Atahuallpa was brought to the place in chains,
with Father Valverde, who had affixed his signature to the
sentence, by his side, actively labouring to convert him
to Christianity, even at the last hour. When the royal
victim was bound to the stake, with the faggots heaped
around him, the Father held up a cross, imploring him
to embrace it and be baptized, and promising that if he
did so the painful death to which he had been sentenced
should be commuted for the milder form of the *garrote*.
This argument proved effectual ; he consented to abjure
his own religion, and receive baptism. The ceremony

EXECUTION OF ATAHUALLPA.

was performed by Valverde, and the new convert received the name of Juan de Atahuallpa. He then expressed his desire that his remains might be interred with those of his maternal ancestors at Quito, and commended his young children to the care and protection of Pizarro. With stern composure he submitted himself to the hands of the executioner, and was suddenly strangled, while the Spanish soldiers around him muttered their *Credos* for the welfare of his soul.* His body that night was exposed in the great square, and on the following morning interred with solemn funeral pomp in the Church of San Franciso. Pizarro and the principal cavaliers attended in mourning garb, and the troops listened attentively to the service read and chanted by Father Valverde. In the middle of it a loud lamentation was heard outside the church, the doors were suddenly burst open, and many Indian women, the wives and sisters of the murdered Inca, swept up the central aisle, and with tears and sobs prostrated themselves around the corpse. They piteously protested that the

* Atahuallpa was of a handsome countenance and fine presence, with blood-shot eyes and a fierce expression, tall, robust, and well proportioned. His air was commanding, but not without a touch of refinement. "He is accused of having been cruel in his wars, and bloody in his revenge. It may be true, but the pencil of an enemy would be likely to overcharge the shadows of the portrait. He is allowed to have been bold, high-minded, and liberal. All agree that he showed singular penetration and quickness of perception. His exploits as a warrior had placed his valour beyond dispute. The best homage to it is the reluctance shown by the Spaniards to restore him to freedom. They dreaded him as an enemy, and they had done him too many wrongs to think that he would be their friend."—*Prescott*, i., 444-45.

funeral rites of their lord should have been celebrated
in the Peruvian fashion, and expressed their desire to
sacrifice themselves on his grave, and accompany his
spirit to the golden land of the Sun. The Spaniards
informed them that Atahuallpa had died in the Christian
religion, and that the God of the Christians required no
human sacrifices. They were then excluded from the
church, but several, on retiring to their residences,
carried out their vows, and by committing suicide confirmed their devotion to the murdered prince.

A day or two later, Hernando de Soto returned ; and
great was his indignation when he was informed of the
cruel deed done in his absence. Repairing at once to
the presence of Pizarro, he found him with a large felt
sombrero, by way of mourning, drawn down over his
eyes, his attitude and bearing suggestive of sorrow, and
perhaps remorse. With a soldier's abruptness, he said
to him : " You have acted rashly, for Atahuallpa was
falsely accused. There was no army at Guamachucho,
nor did I anywhere see the signs of insurrection. If it
were necessary to bring the Inca to trial, he should have
been sent to Castile, to be judged by the Emperor. I
would have pledged myself to have seen him safely on
board ship." Pizarro acknowledged his precipitancy,
and threw all the blame on Riquelme, Valverde, and
the more pertinacious members of the majority, who, in
their turn, recriminated against Pizarro. The quarrel
was loud, violent, and prolonged ; but as they could not
bring the dead back to life, the contending parties at
length subsided into silence.

Pizarro's next step was to name a successor to the late Inca, and after some consideration he selected a younger brother of Atahuallpa, who was accordingly crowned with the royal *borla*, and received the homage of such Indians as remained in or about Caxamalca. Pizarro probably hoped that a young man without experience, owing the crown to his favour and support, would prove a plastic and willing instrument in his hand; while the task of government would be rendered much easier if apparently sanctioned by that supreme authority so long an object of reverence to the Peruvians. On the other hand, the people of Cuzco and the surrounding country acknowledged Manco Capac, a brother of Huascar. To neither belonged that absolute power which the sovereigns of Peru had previously enjoyed; for the captivity and death of Atahuallpa had broken up the old order before a new one was ready to take its place, and the bonds of allegiance in the various provinces had been loosened, if not dissolved. So many of the royal house had been put to death by Atahuallpa, that not only had their influence in the state diminished with their number, but the veneration attaching to a supposed sacred race had considerably decreased. Hence it arose that in different parts of the empire men of ambition seized upon as much authority as their resources permitted, and exercised a jurisdiction to which they had no claim. In Quito, Ruminavi, the late Inca's chief commander, arrested the brother and children of his unfortunate sovereign, slew them without pity, and refusing allegiance to Toparca and Manco

Capac alike, endeavoured to form an independent kingdom.

One sad consequence of this sudden revolution was the moral disorder which speedily convulsed the state. Relieved from the heavy pressure of the Inca's power, the Indians gave way to the most violent excesses. Villages were burnt, palaces and temples were pillaged and destroyed ; their treasures wasted, scattered, or concealed. The Peruvian attributed a new importance to the precious metals when he saw the value put upon them by his conquerors; and thus a simple-minded pastoral community was suddenly infected with the greed of gain. Formerly reserved for religious decoration or state purposes, gold and silver were now regarded as private property, and hoarded up and buried in caves and forests. The amount secreted by the natives is supposed to have largely exceeded that which fell into the hands of the Spaniards. "What the Inca gave the Spaniards," said some of the Indian nobles to Benalcazar, the conqueror of Quito, "was but as a grain of corn compared with the heap before him."

Recognizing that he had no longer to deal with an organized and united state, but with a community broken violently asunder by the disappearance of the authority which had held it together and formed its strength, Pizarro prepared to continue and complete the work of conquest. He had at his disposal a force of nearly 500 veteran soldiers, of whom 160 were horsemen. They were well-equipped, inured to adventure, and full of spirit. At their head, early in September, he set out from Caxamalca, which he left in charge of a sufficient garrison. His route lay along the magnificent causeway which crossed the slopes of the Cordilleras to the ancient city of Cuzco. In the van of his little army he rode triumphantly, mounted on a noble white charger; and at a short distance behind came two superb litters, bearing Toparea and Chilicuchima, each surrounded by his usual attendants. Next followed the Spanish horsemen on their prancing steeds—stalwart men were they, with all the true Spaniard's pride of port—and the sun glancing brightly from their shining shields and polished helms, they made a gallant show. But scarcely less brave the appearance of the infantry in their steel cuirasses, as, with bow or arquebuse in hand, or massive pike, they marched along with solid, steady tramp. The rear was brought up by a crowd of Peruvians, men and women, who acted as guides, servants, or baggage-porters.

The great road of the Incas carried them easily across smooth and level valleys, dotted with prosperous villages and brightened by crystal streams,—over elevated plains that breathed a fresh pure air, and commanded glorious views of the sea on one hand, and the white masses of the mountains on the other,—around precipitous cliffs which seemed ready to crush the daring traveller with their nodding crags,—through wooded gorges, where at mid-noon a twilight obscurity prevailed,—and down descents which, but for this wonderful paved causeway, must have been impassable to cavalry. It was when the road climbed the mountain-side in steep zig-zags, almost resembling a tier of steps, that the horsemen found their progress difficult, and were compelled to dismount and lead their chargers by the bridle. Every evening, when the army halted, they found ample supplies prepared for them, and convenient shelter. Hence there was little suffering, except when they crossed the rough pinnacles of the Cordilleras, and breathed the different air of the iced mountain-tops. Then they underwent some inconvenience from the cold; for, in order that they might march more quickly, they had left all superfluous baggage, and even their huts, at Caxamalca. The bleak blasts penetrated the stout harness of the soldiers; but the poor Indians of the plains, accustomed to a warm soft climate, and scantily clothed, suffered most severely. The rude experiences through which the Spanish veterans had passed seemed to have hardened them, body and mind.

The Spaniards met with no molestation from the enemy. As they marched along, the peasantry came forth to see them, but their impulse was curiosity rather than hatred. Occasionally, however, they came upon ruined bridges and the blackened remains of burned villages; and the Indian scouts brought Pizarro word of small bodies of the natives, armed, hovering on his track, or lying concealed in the ravines and the covert of the woods. It was not until he reached Xauxa that he met with any show of opposition. A Peruvian force, posted on the opposite bank of the river, prepared to dispute his passage; but the Spaniards plunged into the water, made their way across, and, with great slaughter, drove their opponents into flight.

Of Xauxa, in connection with Hernando Pizarro's visit, we have already spoken. "It was seated," says Prescott, "in the midst of a verdant valley, fertilized by a thousand little rills, which the thrifty Indian husbandman drew from the parent river that rolled sluggishly through the meadows. There were several capacious buildings of rough stone in the town, and a temple of some note in the times of the Incas. But the strong arm of Father Valverde and his countrymen soon tumbled the heathen deities from their pride of place, and established in their stead the sacred effigies of the Virgin and Child."

Pizarro halted here to found a Spanish colony, for which the site was favourable. Meanwhile he despatched De Soto, with sixty horsemen, to explore the road to Cuzco, and restore such bridges as he found demolished. As he advanced he found the people more prompt to manifest their hatred of the strangers ; and at Bilcas, in a mountain defile, was engaged in a sharp struggle, which cost him the lives of two or three of his troopers. A fierce contest awaited him in the pass of Vilcaconga, across the river Apurimac. Caught in an ambush, he and his men were called upon to fight for dear life ; from cavern and thicket the enemy issued, with loud shouts of war, and poured in upon them a storm of missiles. Men and horses were toppled over in the fury of the onset ; and the foremost files, retiring on those not yet up the ascent, spread disorder and destruction in their ranks. In vain De Soto endeavoured to rally them ; their horses were confused and maddened by the incessant missiles, and in vain endeavoured to free themselves from the enemy, who clung desperately to their limbs. In the distance rose a broad and open bit of tableland. De Soto saw that his only hope of safety lay in reaching it. Clasping his helmet and lowering his spear, he struck his spurs deep into his horse's flanks, shouted the old battle-cry of Spain, and followed and supported by his men, cut his way right through the swarm of dusky warriors and gained the level beyond.

Then both parties paused, as if by signal, to take a moment's breathing-time ; and the Spaniards hastened to water their horses in a stream that flowed close by. Again De Soto galloped to the charge; again the Indians received it with admirable steadiness, showing no dismay even at the appearance of the snorting, trampling, furious horses ; and it was night alone that put an end to the fighting. Both sides withdrawing from the ground, they took up their stations within an easy distance of each other, so that in the hush of the night they could clearly hear each others' voices. The two armies looked forward with very different feelings to a renewal of the fight on the morrow. The Spaniards were discouraged and alarmed by a strength and steadiness of resistance which they had never expected. They had lost some of their bravest cavaliers; one by a blow from a Peruvian battle-axe, which had cloven his skull from the crown to the chin, thus attesting the excellence of the weapon and the strength of the arm that wielded it. Several horses had been killed ; few, either of the men or horses, had escaped without a wound; and the Indian allies had suffered still more severely.

From the orderliness and steadiness of the assault De
Soto concluded it had been directed by some experienced chief,—perhaps by the Indian commander Quizquiz, who was reputed to be in that neighbourhood with
a considerable army.   The Spaniard, however, did his
best to raise the spirits of his men ; reminding them
that though weary with a long march, and their horses
exhausted, they had kept the enemy at bay, and that,
refreshed by a night's rest, they might confidently hope
to turn the tide of battle on the morrow; reminding
them also " to trust in the Almighty, who would never
desert His faithful followers in their extremity."

And so it proved, for Pizarro, having information of
the dangerous state of the country, and the rapid gathering of bodies of armed Indians, had grown alarmed for
the safety of his lieutenant.   Accordingly he sent forward
Almagro, with the bulk of the remaining cavalry, to
support and succour him ; and he, advancing by forced
marches, reached the foot of the Vi'caconga river on
the very night of the engagement.   From his spies he
heard of the day's fighting, and though his horses were
blown and weary he pushed forward to find De Soto.
The night was densely dark ; and to apprise his comrade
of his approach, he sounded his trumpets on the march.
Cheerily their martial notes rang through the defiles,
and, repeated by the mountain echoes, infused fresh
courage into the heart of every battle-worn cavalier, while
De Soto's silver bugles pealed a shrill reply.   Before the
day dawned the two companies of Spaniards were united.

By the morning light the Peruvians saw their extended

array, and dismayed by its strength, took advantage of
the heavy mist which hung about the mountains to
accomplish their retreat. Almagro and De Soto then
continued their march until they cleared the defiles of
the mountains, when, entrenching themselves in a strong
position, they awaited the arrival of Pizarro.

Pizarro, on receiving information of their safety, rejoiced
exceedingly; and, in the true Crusader spirit,* caused
mass to be said and thanksgiving made, because heaven
had showered its favours upon the Christians throughout
the mighty enterprise. It seemed certain that the attack
on De Soto's party had been organized and directed by
some man of authority; and suspicion fell upon the
veteran Chilicuchima, who was believed to maintain a
secret correspondence with Quizquiz. Pizarro hastened
to accuse him of the conspiracy, reproaching him with
ingratitude towards the Spaniards, who had treated him
with so much liberality, and assuring him, with a s'ern
frown, that if he did not cause the Peruvians to lay down
their arms at once, he should be burnt alive so soon as
they reached Almagro's encampment.

The aged chief coldly replied that he knew of no conspiracy, and that so long as he remained a prisoner he
could have no influence over his countrymen. Pizarro
then ordered him to be put in irons, and placed a strong
guard over him.

* Pizarro and his men were scarcely less Crusaders than gold-
hunters. They were impelled by a strange medley of motives;
some, mean and worldly; others, noble and spiritual; a greed of
gain, a love of adventure, a lust of power, and a desire to convert
the heathen to Christianity.

Before setting out from Xauxa Pizarro sustained a new misfortune in the death of Toparca, the young Inca. It was the result, apparently, of the prince's continued brooding over the sorrows of his race and dynasty, but the Spaniards attributed it to the machinations of Chilicuchima.*

Leaving a garrison of forty men to guard his treasure in Xauxa, and defend the town against any Peruvian attack, Pizarro marched to effect a junction with Almagro and De Soto, and with his united forces entered the vale of Xaquixaguama, about five leagues from Cuzco. "This," we are told, "was one of those bright spots so often found embosomed amidst the Andes,—the more beautiful from contrast with the savage character of the scenery around it. A river flowed through the valley, affording the means of irrigating the soil, and clothing it in perpetual verdure; and the rich and flowering vegetation spread out like a cultivated garden. The beauty of the place and its delicious coolness commended it as a residence for the Peruvian nobles, and the sides of the hills were dotted with their villas, which afforded them a grateful retreat in the heats of summer. Yet the centre of the valley was disfigured by a quagmire of some extent, occasioned by the frequent overflowing of the waters; but the industry of the Indian architects had constructed a solid causeway, faced with heavy stone, and connected with the great road, which traversed the whole breadth of the morass."

* The allegation that he died of chagrin at the subordinate position in which Pizarro placed him is made by Velasco (of Quito). and by no other writer.

I

Here Pizarro halted and refreshed his troops. Here, too, he brought Chilicuchima to trial—if trial that mockery could be called, in which the judge and accuser were one, and the sentence was decided upon before the evidence was heard or the prisoner's guilt established. He was condemned to be burnt alive.* "Some thought it a hard measure," remarks Herrera; "but those who are governed by reasons of state policy are apt to shut their eyes against everything else." The sole reason of state policy that could have impelled Pizarro to commit this indefensible act must have been his determination not to leave the Peruvians with any man of authority or eminence to act as their leader and rally them against their oppressors. With his usual anxiety to save the souls of those who fell victims to Spanish greed or fear, Father Valverde accompanied Chilicuchima to the stake, and pressed upon him the arguments always at his command in favour of conversion : through the waters of baptism he would pass into the bliss of Paradise. Chili-cuchima simply replied, "I do not understand the religion of the white man ; " nor, as it was practised by the conquerors and their priest,† could he be expected to do so. He suffered death with unaffected heroism ;

---

* Mr. Prescott does not see why the Spanish conquerors so often resorted to this cruel mode of execution. Because, I suppose, they looked upon the Peruvians as heretics, and death by fire was, in Spain, the traditional punishment of heresy.

† The inferiority of Valverde, in character and conduct, to the wise and humane chaplain of Cortes needs no comment. A similar inferiority is stamped upon all the personages connected with the conquest of Peru.

neither sigh nor groan escaped him, and with his last breath he uttered the sacred name of Pachacamác. His followers endeavoured to shorten his tortures by piling fresh fuel on the faggots which blazed around him.

A few days later, and the Spanish camp was surprised by the appearance of a young Peruvian noble, richly attired, surrounded by great pomp, and attended by a gorgeous retinue. This was Manco Capac, brother of the unfortunate Huascar, and the sole legitimate claimant of the *borla* of the Incas. Finding it impossible to stay the progress of the invaders, he politicly claimed their protection ; and after asserting his title to the throne, he solicited the aid of Pizarro in securing it. The Spanish commander was well pleased to act with the sanction of a native prince ; the death of Toparca he had felt as a serious misfortune, and he, therefore, received Manco with an unaffected and eager cordiality, assuring him that the King of Spain had sent him to Peru for the special purpose of vindicating Huascar's claim to the throne, and chastising his rival.

With the young Inca and his attendants in his train, Pizarro advanced upon Cuzco. In passing through the mountain-defile that forms the approach, he encountered a body of the Peruvians, whom, after a sharp contest, he beat off, and towards sunset his army debouched on the green slope in front of the ancient city. Beautiful it looked as it lay in the purple and golden splendours of the setting sun,—the great luminary to whose worship it was consecrated,—with the shadowy forms of the mountains holding it in their soft embrace. Pizarro deferred his entry until the following day, the anniversary of his entry into Caxamalca, November 15th, 1533. Vigilant watch was kept during the night, lest a surprise should be attempted; and early in the morning Pizarro drew up his little army in three divisions, placing himself at the head of the centre, with De Soto and his brilliant horsemen in the van. Then with banners waving and trumpets blaring victoriously, with the sheen of arms and the flutter of plumes and the tramp of steeds, he passed through the gates of the City of the Sun, and filed into its principal street. All along the route were assembled crowds of Peruvians, dressed in their many-coloured costume, and wearing their distinctive head-gear, which, by its fashion, indicated the province from which they came. They gazed with silent wonder at the Spaniards as at a mysterious race of beings, whose origin it was impossible to determine; the arms, the shining armour, the white complexions, the firm and martial tread, the military music, the neigh and clatter of the horses, all moved their curiosity, perhaps their dread; but they broke into loud acclamations when their young prince appeared in his sumptuous litter, borne by the side of the Spanish general. To Spaniards and Peruvians alike the spectacle must have presented the strangest features. In the contact of the Old World with the New, of the higher and more developed with the lower and more imperfect civilization, there was always much to interest; but its deeper meanings would not be apprehended by any of those who took part in the scene as actors or spectators. They would remark only its external and

more obvious characters, which, indeed, were striking
enough and numerous enough to attract and reward
attention.

Pizarro made directly for the great square, in order to
secure a strong defensive position for his troops. It was
surrounded by several low ranges of buildings, including
the palaces of the Incas, and in one of these, which was
surmounted by a tower, he took up his quarters, and
provided lodgings for his officers. The soldiers were
encamped, at least for the first few weeks, in their tents in
the broad open *plaza*, which was neatly paved with pebbles;
and their horses were picketed by their side. Without
delay the great banner of Spain was hoisted on the ramparts of the fortress,—which was built of hewn st ne on
a rocky height dominating the city,—on the palaces,
and on the Temple of the Sun ; a sign to all who looked
upon it of the lost independence of the kingdom of the
Incas. For the administration of the city, Pizarro made
the necessary arrangements ;* but at this time the con-
tentment and tranquillity of the inhabitants were such
as to relieve him from all anxiety. He wisely prohibited
the soldiery from entering the houses of the people, but
they were allowed to plunder the temples and palaces
of their decorations. They even despoiled of their gems
and ornaments the royal mummies in the temple of
Coricancha ; for vast as was the treasure of Cuzco, it

---

* He assumed for himself the office of " Governor," and created a
kind of supreme magistracy or civil jurisdiction (the eight *Regidores*),
of which two of his brothers were members (Gonzalo and Juan),
March 24th, 1534.

did not come up to the extravagant anticipations of the
Spaniards. In some instances they tortured the inhabitants to wring from them a confession of the places in
which they had concealed their wealth. They disturbed
the repose of the dead, and spoiled the graves of the
precious articles which household affection had deposited
there. No expedient was omitted, no place left unex-
plored, that promised to swell the total of their booty.
When all was collected, the greediest among them had
no cause to be dissatisfied. There were vases of pure
gold, beautifully wrought; plates and bars of gold, four
golden llamas, and ten or twelve female figures made of
fine gold, as large as life, and as beautiful and well-
proportioned as if they had been alive. There were also
bars of solid silver, richly tinted robes of cotton and
feather-work, slippers and sandals of gold, and women's
dresses composed entirely of golden beads. When the
gold was all melted down, and the division made—after
the King's fifth and the shares of Pizarro and Almagro
had been reserved—each horse-soldier received six thousand pesos of gold, and each infantry-soldier half that
sum.*

This splendid booty, added to the spoil divided at
Caxamalca, elevated the commonest soldier to the position of a millionaire; but it was of little benefit except
to the sober-minded and prudent individuals, who, contented with so splendid a reward of their labours, withdrew

---

* Sancho, who succeeded Xeres as Pizarro's secretary, estimates
the whole amount at 580,200 pesos of gold. and 215 000 marks of
silver, which would give a smaller share to each soldier.

from the enterprise, and returned to Spain to enjoy it in tranquillity.*

This delicate matter of the distribution of the booty being satisfactorily settled,—and its fairness seems to have been universally acknowledged,—Pizarro's next care was to obtain a national recognition of Manco Capac as the lawful sovereign of Peru. He accordingly caused him to be publicly invested with the *borla*, observing all the traditional ceremonies, and celebrating the event with all the ancient pageantry. He and the young prince pledged each other in goblets of *chica ;* the mummies of the dead Incas were paraded through the public square, each with its gorgeous retinue, and seated in its place at the banquet-table ; with dances and songs and feasts the populace were entertained most lavishly. But

* Prescott says : " The sudden influx of so much wealth, and that, too, in so transferable a form, among a party of reckless adventurers little accustomed to the possession of money, had its natural effect. It supplied them with the means of gaming, so strong and common a passion with the Spaniards that it may be considered a national vice. Fortunes were lost and won in a single day, sufficient to render the proprietors independent for life ; and many a desperate gamester, by an unlucky throw of the dice or turn of the cards, saw himself stripped in a few hours of the fruits of years of toil, and obliged to begin over again the business of rapine. Among these, one in the cavalry service is mentioned, named Leguizano, who had received as his share of the booty the image of the Sun, which, raised on a plate of burnished gold, spread over the walls in a recess of the great temple, and which, for some reason or other,—perhaps because of its superior fineness,—was not recast like the other ornaments. This rich prize the spendthrift lost in a single night ; whence it came to be a proverb in Spain, *Juega el Sol antes que amanezca*, ' Play away the Sun before sunrise.' "— *History of the Conquest of Peru*, i., 479.

at least *one* novel feature was introduced, which to a proud people would have communicated a deep pang. The royal notary read a formal assertion of the supremacy of the house of Castile, and required its acknowledgment by all present. The act of homage was then performed by each person waving the royal banner of Castile twice or thrice with his hands. We may conjecture that while thus publicly proclaiming his dependence, the young Inca was secretly resolving to throw off the yoke at the earliest possible opportunity.

The Spanish Governor, when the festivities were concluded, was at leisure to complete the organisation of his conquest; and, unlettered as he was, his strong natural intellect enabled him to do his work well and thoroughly. To secure the settlement of a sufficient number of Spaniards, he liberally distributed the houses and lands he had confiscated from the Incas. He provided for the police and good order of the city. The interests of religion occupied him largely. In the great *plaza* he laid the foundation of a stately cathedral. On the site of the once splendid Temple of the Sun rose a spacious monastery; and the House of the Virgins of the Sun was replaced by a Roman Catholic nunnery. He encouraged the Fathers of St. Dominic and other missionaries in their zealous, if not always well-conceived, exertions for the conversion of the people; so that schools, and churches, and monasteries sprang up with wonderful rapidity.

From these peaceful labours, in which the conqueror is seen at his best,—prudent, moderate, and far-seeing,—he was called away by the efforts of some of the bolder Peruvian captains to arrest and even turn back the tide of Spanish conquest. A considerable force, under Quizquiz, had concentrated in the neighbourhood of Cuzco. Pizarro sent against them some squadrons under Almagro, and a large body of Peruvians under the young Inca, who, as the soldiers of Quizquiz belonged to the Atahuallpa faction, readily took part in the expedition. Almagro acted with his usual promptitude and decision. By swift marches he surprised the hostile camp; by repeated blows he drove the enemy back upon Xauxa ; where he fought a great battle, which, like all previous encounters between the natives and their invaders, ended in the total defeat of the former. Quizquiz fled to the tablelands of Quito, and his own soldiers, weary of a campaign in which they suffered heavily, and gained not even honour, put him to death.

A greater danger than any hostile demonstration of the Peruvians next threatened the conquerors ; for it seemed to involve the possibility of a hazardous contention with their own countrymen. The reader acquainted with the enterprise of Cortes and the conquest of Mexico will remember that one of his boldest lieutenants was Don Pedro de Alvarado, and that he was rewarded for his services with the appointment of Governor of Guatemala. To this restless and aspiring warrior rumour bore the tidings of Pizarro's success in Peru, and of the apparently unlimited wealth which his fortunate sword had won. Both his ambition and his avarice were stimulated by the news; and understanding that the expedition of

Pizarro had been confined to Peru, he resolved on the conquest of Quito, which, as Atahuallpa's early residence and inheritance, might be supposed to abound in treasure. He justified his design by the pretence that Quito lay within the borders of his province of Guatemala. Levying volunteers and preparing a large fleet, he sailed for the Bay of Caraques, where, in March 1534, he landed with the finest army that had yet been seen in the New World—an army consisting of 270 foot, and no fewer than 230 horse, all splendidly equipped.

At the outset, however, he blundered. It was a necessity that he should take a route different to that of Pizarro, and he determined on crossing the mountain by the direct path ; a passage which, even in the best season—and Alvarado had not chosen the best season—is one of formidable difficulty. Deserted by his native guide, he plunged into the recesses of the Cordilleras, and ascended those frozen heights in a painful and laborious march. Caught in violent storms of snow and hail, his soldiers, accustomed to the warm climate of Guatemala, suffered terribly ; and their Indian attendants, still less fitted to endure excessive cold, perished by hundreds. The horsemen were frozen in their saddles, rigid as statues. The infantry could scarcely drag their benumbed limbs over the rugged ground and through the accumulating drifts. Their provisions failed them, and they disputed eagerly with the condors for the carcases of their exhausted and half-famished horses. When Alvarado descended the other side of the fatal heights, into a milder atmosphere, his once splendid army was reduced by three-fourths, and he had only a few horses left.

As soon as Pizarro was apprised of Alvarado's expedition, he despatched Almagro to encounter it. He could spare him only a small company, but he was directed to proceed by San Miguel, and to reinforce himself with a portion of its garrison. On reaching San Miguel, he was dismayed to learn that the commander, Benalcazar, had started on an expedition of his own. He, too, had been fired by the stories which reached him of the riches of Quito, and with a hundred and forty soldiers, and some Indian auxiliaries, had undertaken its conquest. Crossing the tableland of Quito, he encountered the Peruvian General, Ruminavi, in the neighbourhood of Riobamba, and after much desperate fighting won a complete victory. Entering the city in triumph, he hoisted the flag of Castile on its walls, and re-named it, in honour of his general, San Francisco del Quito; but, to his intense mortification, he found that its treasures had been removed, or had existed only in fiction. Meantime Almagro had rapidly followed in his track, his fiery spirit unquenched by the snows of nearly seventy winters. He was several times opposed by the Indians, but his impetuous courage scattered them in every direction, and at Riobamba he united his little company with Benalcazar's force. Then he awaited the approach of Alvarado. The latter, as we have seen, had undergone grievous misfortunes; and when he found himself opposed by a veteran soldier like Almagro, showed a manifest disposition to treat rather than to fight. His men also, mixing with their compatriots, and hearing glowing reports of the beauty and wealth of Cuzco, were inclined to abandon his standard, and rally to Pizarro's. In these circumstances the task of Almagro was easy, and he offered Alvarado a sum of 100,000 pesos, on condition that he made over his ships, troops, and supplies. The offer was not exceptionally liberal, but Alvarado accepted it ; and the negotiation depended only on the approval of Pizarro.

The Governor, leaving his brother Juan, with ninety men, in charge of Cuzco, moved forward to meet Almagro and Alvarado, who had descended to the sea-coast, and in the valley of Pachacamác the three Spanish commanders came together. Pizarro instantly confirmed the agreement made by his colleague, and the stipulated sum was duly paid. After a merry round of chivalrous pastimes and sumptuous banquets, Alvarado re-embarked for his government of Guatemala, and Almagro departed to take the government of Cuzco. Pizarro was thus at liberty to determine on the site of the future capital of the great empire which he had conquered for the crown of Spain. His sagacity perceived that Cuzco, hidden among the mountains, was too remote from the coast to become the centre of a commerce which must be exclusively conducted by sea. On the other hand, San Miguel was too far north. What was wanted was a site well sheltered, well provided with water, in a fertile country, and of easy access to merchant-vessels ; and such a site he found in the valley of Rimac, or, as the Spaniards called it, Lima, where a broad river, at a distance of two leagues only from the sea, expanded into a noble tidal estuary, forming a natural harbour of the most commodious character. Its central position afforded it an easy communication with all parts of the country. Its climate was soft, equable, and temperate; for, though only twelve degrees from the Equator, it was refreshed and invigorated by the south-west breezes from the Pacific, or the colder currents that swept down the snowy sides of the Cordilleras. And, finally, the slopes on either side were crowned with fertility, and the surrounding scenery mingled the elements of the sublime, the beautiful, and the picturesque.

On the Epiphany festival, January 6th, 1535, Pizarro laid the foundation of his new capital, which he christened *Ciudad de los Reyes*, or the City of the Kings. His contemporaries, however, preferred the modified Indian name, which posterity also has accepted, and it is as Lima that this beautiful city still figures in the map of the world. He laid it out on a plan of almost mathematical symmetry. The general outline was that of a triangle, the base of which was the river, whose healthful waters were, by means of stone conduits, to be distributed through all the principal streets. These streets were of ample width, and intersected each other at right angles; they were so contrived as to afford space for a large garden to every house, and for public squares. Almost in the centre was defined the *plaza*, which was to be surrounded by the cathedral, the palace of the governor, the palace of the municipality, and other public buildings, the foundations in every case being constructed with a solidity that has defied "the assaults of time," and even the more formidable shock of earthquakes. The whole was surrounded by a massive wall of sun-burnt clay, twelve feet high and ten feet thick; and a bridge of five arches was thrown across the river Rimac.

Pizarro pressed forward the work with all his energy. He delighted in it. Advancing years had tempered his martial ardour; success had satisfied his adventurous spirit; and he was fain to crown his career with the " victories of peace." He felt that in this fair new city he was erecting a permanent monument of his fame; and he urged his labourers to redouble their toil by his rewards and encouragements. From a distance of more than a hundred miles he collected his Indian workers; and the Spaniards also laid by the sword, and took up the spade, the pickaxe, or the mason's trowel. In the superintendence of this peaceful enterprise he was inter-rupted, however, by ill news from Cuzco. We have recorded the departure of Hernando Pizarro to Spain, with the King's fifth of the booty of Peru. On his arrival at the Spanish Court, the conqueror was received with a cordial welcome. The tale he had to tell, and the gold he brought, secured him a favourable hearing from Charles V., who willingly granted to Pizarro all the concessions he had asked. The governorship of Peru was bestowed upon Francisco Pizarro, with leave and licence to make conquests two hundred miles further southward. Father Valverde was created Bishop of Cuzco. Hernando himself was made a knight of Santiago, and an officer of the royal Court. Nor was Almagro forgotten.

At Hernando's instigation, he was empowered to discover and occupy the American mainland for a distance of two hundred leagues from the southern limit of Pizarro's territory. Finally, Pizarro was made a Marquis; and the Emperor with his own hand addressed a letter to the two great captains, praising their prowess, and acknowledging their services.

With a large and well-equipped armament, Hernando, towards the end of 1534, sailed from the coast of Spain. He reached Nombre de Dios in safety, but no preparation had been made for his coming, and much time was wasted in collecting the necessary supplies before he could cross the mountains, and hasten to rejoin his brother. Meanwhile his forces suffered much from want and disease; many perished; others, weary of the delay, made their way across the isthmus and into the Peruvian territory. Among these was an agent of Almagro, who overtook him as he was entering Cuzco, and acquainted him with the grant made to him by his sovereign. Pizarro's brothers, in deference to his command, immediately resigned the government of Cuzco to the Mariscal (as he was thenceforth styled); but, inflated by his new authority, the latter at once declared that, by virtue of the royal grant, Cuzco fell within his jurisdiction, and asserted his sole right to it. This was not the case, as the Emperor had considerably extended the boundaries of Pizarro's government; but the full despatches had not as yet arrived, and Almagro acted on his agent's assumption. When the Governor was informed of his comrade's usurpation, he sent instructions to his brothers to resume

K

the government of the city ; and a bitter feud broke out, dividing the soldiers, the civilians, and even the Indian population into two factions, which evinced a disposition to settle their respective pretensions by the arbitrament of the sword.

CHAPTER V.

IZARRO marched at once to Cuzco, where the Spaniards and natives alike received him with a cordial welcome. In his conduct towards the frank and impetuous Almagro he showed a consummate prudence, and avoided any occasion of quarrel. He treated the possession of Cuzco as a question that could not be discussed until both parties had before them the Emperor's despatches; and urged Almagro, while it was in abeyance, to carry his conquering sword southward into the territory of Chili. The influence of some common friends seconded his efforts to prevent a rupture; and at length the agreement between him and Almagro was renewed, and confirmed "with an oath and great affirmations," though there were not wanting stipulations that betrayed their secret distrusts. Thus it was provided that neither of the contracting parties, in their communications to the Emperor, should slander or disparage the other; and that neither should correspond with the Spanish Government without the other's knowledge. In conclusion, they supplicated the anger of heaven against the one which should first violate the solemn bond, invoking upon his head the most terrible punishment, the destruction of his family and property in this life, and in the next the ruin of his soul.* The whole was formally recorded by the notary, and attested by two witnesses, on the 12th of June, 1535. The sanction of religion was also obtained, Almagro and Pizarro partaking of the Host as administered to them by Father Bartolomé de Segovia. The permanence of a compact may well be doubted when the parties to it are evidently so conscious that their interest lies in its disruption.

Shortly afterwards Almagro set out on his enterprise against Chili,† and Pizarro returned to his peaceful and prosperous labours at Lima. He planted several other settlements along the Pacific coast, always at points which indicated his keen intelligence in the selection of them; one, in honour of his birthplace, he named Truxillo. He continued also the process of dividing lands and Indians among his followers, invariably insisting on their humane and generous treatment of the

---

* "Con todo rigor de justicia permita la perdicion de su anima."

† Before he went he strongly recommended Pizarro to send his brothers back to Castile, insisting on their imperious manners and hasty tempers, and expressing his willingness that out of the joint treasure Pizarro should compensate them as liberally as he pleased. The Governor, however, knew that they were faithful, and he answered that they respected and loved him like a father, and would give no occasion of offence.

Indians, and making their religious instruction a special duty. While he was thus engaged, a wholly unexpected event aroused the fears of the Spaniards. To all outward seeming the conquest of Peru was complete, and its inhabitants apparently acquiesced in the revolution that had taken place, a revolution which had destroyed their independence, broken up their social system, degraded their religion, and wrecked their liberties. The Inca himself was virtually a prisoner in Spanish hands, mocked with the shadow of power, compelled to move like a puppet at the bidding of his master. The Spaniards, therefore, were under little alarm as to any national insurrection, especially after the defeat of the Indian generals Quizquiz and Ruminavi. The keener was their surprise, and the more profound their indignation, when a formidable revolt broke out towards the end of April 1536.

It was soon after the departure of Almagro for the south that Hernando Pizarro, having overcome his difficulties at Nombre de Dios, arrived at Lima with the despatches from the King of Spain (July 1535). These conclusively proved that Cuzco was within the Peruvian territory, or Nuevo Castilla, as the Spaniards called it, and under the authority of Pizarro. In return for the Imperial favours, Hernando had prom'sed to raise in Nuevo Castilla a voluntary contribution, or benevolence, towards the expenses of the Emperor's wars; but he soon discovered that the Spanish settlers and soldiers were wholly averse to any such costly manifestation of loyalty. They had regularly paid their fifths, and was not that enough? Hernando shrewdly replied that they had paid them out of the ransom of Atahuallpa, and that, as he was a royal person, his ransom of right belonged to the Emperor. Eventually, by a dexterous employment of persuasion, entreaty, and menace, the Marquis raised nearly the amount required; and to complete it he sent Hernando to replace his brother Juan in the government of Cuzco, and levy a contribution.

On his arrival at Cuzco, Hernando found both his brothers, Juan and Gonzalo, absent on an expedition to subdue some refractory chiefs. When they returned, he brought the subject of the benevolence before the municipality, and by the application of considerable pressure succeeded in extracting a certain amount of gold. He was engaged in melting it down, when news arrived of an outbreak in the district of Collao, and of the return of Villacma, the high priest who had accompanied Almagro's expedition. Hernando immediately inquired of the Inca if the news were true; and was answered in the affirmative. The Inca added that Villacma had returned because he had been sorely ill-treated by Almagro's followers, and he asked Pizarro's permission to go forth from the city to meet him. This was granted; the two great Peruvians met, and returned together to Cuzco, to discourse upon their common causes of discomfort, and to meditate upon the chances of a successful outbreak. Ignorant of the conspiracy that was being nursed, Hernando readily gave his consent when the Inca and some of his chiefs solicited permission to repair to the valley of Yucay to celebrate certain ceremonies in memory of his illustrious father, Huayna Capac, who was there interred. On the 18th of April, 1536, the Inca, accompanied by Villacma, quitted Cuzco, ostensibly on this pious errand. Two days elapsed, and a Spaniard from the country brought the surprising intelligence that the Inca, instead of going to Yucay, had gone to Ares, about forty miles distant, among the mountains, and that he suspected him of a design to revolt. Hernando paid no attention to this warning, but sent a messenger after the Inca to request him to hasten his return, that he might accompany him on an expedition to chastise the rebellious caciques of Collao. The Inca, however, in his mountain fastnesses, could treat the Spaniard's message with contempt, and reveal the noble design he entertained of delivering his country from the burden of foreign oppression. He assembled the chiefs and principal persons of the surrounding district; made a vigorous appeal to their patriotism, their loyalty, their religious sentiment; spoke to them, we can hardly doubt, of their violated altars, of their plundered hearths, of the wrongs done to their wives, their daughters, their sisters; of the insults levelled at their priests, and the pollution inflicted on the sacred virgins of the Sun; and then, two large golden vessels brimful of wine being placed before them, he exclaimed : " I am resolved not to leave a Christian alive in all this land, and therefore in the first place I shall lay siege to Cuzco. Whoever amongst you will serve me in this must stake his life upon it. Drink !"*

* " Yo estoi determinado de no dexar Cristiano á vida en toda a tierra, y para este quiero primero poner cereo en el Cuzco. Quien de vosotros pensare servirme en este, ha de poner sobre val caso la vida. Beva."—VICENTE DE VALVERDE.

A few words may here be said in description of the
city which witnessed the last scene in the tragic drama
of the Peruvian conquest. It was constructed on a
plan of extraordinary regularity, which probably suggested
to Pizarro the plan of Lima. The streets intersected one
another at right angles, so that the blocks of buildings
formed perfect parallelograms. Each street was refreshed
by a large stone conduit of water passing through its
centre. There was a great square, of which the principal
feature was the palace of the late Inca, Huayna Capac,
with its gateway of many-coloured marbles; a palace so
extensive that it afterwards provided quarters for the
chief among the Spanish "conquistadors." Adjacent to
it were three other palaces, with painted fronts and a
profusion of sculptured decoration. Three sides of the
square were lined by covered buildings, like arcades, in
which the great state festivals and religious ceremonies
were celebrated during bad weather. The city was
divided into four quarters, corresponding to the four
provinces of the empire;* and when the men of any
particular province came up to Cuzco, they were required to assemble in the outskirts of their proper quarter.

Most of the houses were built of stone; some of bricks
burnt in the sun. The roofs were covered with wooden
tiles thatched with rush-work. In the poorer streets were
houses built of clay and reeds. Numerous squares and
spacious openings served as the lungs of the city, and,
by admitting an ample volume of fresh air, favoured the
public health.

* Antisuyo, Chinchasuyo, Collasuyo, Condesuyo.

Two streams, entering the city under bridges provided with flood-gates, traversed its entire extent in artificial channels, lined and paved with masonry.

Towards the north, on a high sierra,* a spur of the mighty Cordillera, rose a strong fortress, the remains of which, to this day, awaken the traveller's wonder. On the side facing the city, where the steepness of the precipice was almost sufficient protection, it was defended by a massive wall, about twelve hundred feet in length. On the other side, where the slope rendered access comparatively easy, it was surrounded by three semicircular walls at a considerable distance from each other, built with salient and retiring angles, twenty-one in number. "On the top of the walls were terraces forming ramparts. These terraces had breastworks, so that the Peruvians could fight almost under cover." The narrowest rampart was of such a width that three carriages could pass abreast.

The fortress itself consisted of three detached towers, arranged in a triangle, the apex of which was occupied by the principal tower, a circular keep of four stories, with ample windows that overlooked the court. This was the Inca's residence, and fitted up with royal splendour. The other two towers were devoted to the accommodation of the garrison, which consisted always of members of the noble families of Peru, commanded by an officer of the blood royal; these towers were rectangular in shape. The three were connected by subterranean galleries, and similar galleries communicated with the city and the palaces of the Inca. The hill, indeed,

* Its name was Sacsahuaman.

was completely honeycombed with galleries and chambers.

Galleries, walls, towers,—all were built of stone, and on a scale of Titanic vastness. The Spaniards said that not even the Bridge of Segovia, or the other buildings which Hercules and the Romans had made, were worthy to be compared to the citadel of Cuzco. The blocks of masonry formed a kind of rustic-work, being rough-hewn except towards the edges, which were finely wrought; they were not arranged in regular courses, but smaller blocks filled up the interstices between the greater. Many of the stones measured as much as thirty-eight feet in length by eighteen feet in breadth, and were six feet thick.*

As soon as he was convinced of the Inca's defection,

* " We are filled with astonishment when we consider that those enormous masses were hewn from their native bed, and fashioned into shape, by a people ignorant of the use of iron ; that they were brought from quarries, from four to fifteen leagues distant, without the aid of beasts of burden; were transported across rivers and ravines, raised to their elevated position on the sierra, and finally adjusted there with the nicest accuracy, without the knowledge of tools and machinery familiar to the European. Twenty thousand men are said to have been employed on this great structure, and fifty years consumed in the building. However this may be, we see in it the workings of a despotism which had the lives and fortunes of its vassals at its absolute disposal, and which, however mild in its general character, esteemed those vassals, when employed in its service, as lightly as the brute animals for which they served as a substitute."—*Prescott*, " History of the Conquest of Peru," i. 16, 17. "An eyewitness says : ' I measured a stone at Tiaguanaco, twenty-eight feet long, eighteen feet broad, and about six feet thick ; but in the wall of the fortress of Cuzco, which is constructed of masonry, there are many stones of much greater size.' It appears from

Hernando despatched his brother Juan, with fifty horse men, on an attempt to recover possession of his person ; but secure among his mountains, Manco was able to baffle the pursuit of the Spaniard, who was speedily recalled to Cuzco to succour his brother. For, from every province the Indians had gathered at their monarch's summons, until around the capital was arrayed a force of not less than two hundred thousand men,—a splendid military spectacle, on which the Spaniards could not but look with admiration, in spite of their consciousness of peril. The plains, the slopes and summits of the mountains, every valley and defile were bright with the pomp of banners and the sheen of spears. Juan and his little company of cavaliers passed through their ranks unmolested,—perhaps because the Peruvians were not unwilling that as many victims as possible should enter

modern research that some of these stones were fifty feet long, twenty-two feet broad, and six feet thick. How they were conveyed thither is a problem which has exercised ingenious men since the conquest. But the works of despotic monarchs of the olden time, who could employ an army to fetch a single stone, have always astonished more civilized nations, accustomed to a reasonable economy in the use of human labour."—*Sir Arthur Helps*, " Spanish Conquest in America," iv., 29. What seems at least as great a problem is the object intended to be served by the construction of such large ramparts, since it does not appear that the kingdom of the Incas was at any time exposed to foreign invasion or civil commotion. Against what enemy was such Cyclopean masonry raised ? In the work itself, however remarkable, there was nothing marvellous. Given an unlimited command of human strength, and an indefinite duration of time, and Stonehenge might be raised to the summit of the Peak ! The Peruvians did not build for a single reign ; the task was taken up by a long succession of generations, and monotonously carried on until completed.

the net prepared for them,—and were eagerly welcomed by Hernando Pizarro, who even with this reinforcement could muster only two hundred horse and foot, besides a thousand Indian auxiliaries ; and the struggle began.

By day it was formidable to look out upon the forest of spears which surrounded the city; but by night the scene was rendered even more imposing by the immense number of watch-fires that blazed on the hill-top and in the valley, as numerous as " the stars of heaven in a cloudless summer night." Just before dawn, the echoes resounded with the clang of the musical instruments of the Peruvians ; after which they began the day's action with volleys of missiles of every description. Among them were burning arrows and red-hot stones wrapped in cotton that had been steeped in some bituminous sub-stance, and these, flashing through the sky like shooting stars, fell upon the thatched roofs and set them on fire. From all parts of the city leaped vivid tongues of flame ; the conflagration spread to the interior of the houses ; and soon over the scene hung a canopy of lurid smoke, which the wind rolled onwards slowly in dusky billows, reddened by the reflection of the sea of fire beneath. The heat became so intense, that the air seemed to choke and scorch like the breath of a volcano.

Pizazzo had posted his men in the great square ; partly under tents, and partly in the palace-hall of the Inca Viracocha, on the present site of the cathedral. Thrice during that first day of combat—Saturday, May 6th—the roof caught fire ; but though the Spaniards made no effort to extingui h it, the flames died out and did but little harm. Therefore there were many devout-minded soldiers willing to ascribe "the miracle" to the intervention of the Blessed Virgin, who had been seen, on white wings upborne, hovering over the spot on which was to be raised a temple to her honour. Happily, the Spanish force sustained no injury from the spreading flames, which could not invade the open area of their encampment; but their spirits were depressed by the dreary spectacle of the burning city, and the shouts and yells of the Indians gathered on the hillsides all around. For several days and nights the flames continued their work of devastation, until one-half the city was a mass of blackened ruins. Palace and hovel, tower and temple, all were destroyed. But among the few large buildings that escaped were the " House of the Sun " and the " House of the Virgins ; " while still the gray fortress on its rocky height rose superior to the menace of peril.

While the conflagration raged the Indians were persistent in their attacks. To prevent the cavalry from charging them they dug holes and raised barricades ; and sometimes with dexterous aim they flung the *lasso* at horse or rider, entangled him in its coil, and brought him to the ground. Under cover of the fire and smoke they made sudden dashes forward, displaying an unexpected courage and impetuosity ; and when they were driven back, fresh battalions poured down into the fight, until it seemed as if the Spaniards must be overwhelmed by sheer weight of numbers. Never in all the annals of chivalry did the Spaniards bear themselves more bravely. Tearing down the barricades, they made a clear path for their horsemen, who rode in among the masses of the enemy and slaughtered them piteously with sword or spear. But they could scarcely hold their ground, and each attack they delivered or repulsed cost them some life they ill could spare. Hernando was the soul of their defence. Wherever the enemy's pressure was greatest, he might be seen, contending in the front of the affray. He hastened from point to point, like one incapable of fatigue ; with a word of encouragement for a comrade, with a deadly stroke for a foe. Bitterly did he regret his want of forethought in not occupying the fortress on the rock, from which the continual showers of missiles added much to the embarrassment of his soldiers; but he allowed no sign of doubt or regret to appear, and fought on as if victory were the inevitable result of the struggle.

It was needful that so firm a soul should maintain the unequal contest, for the rumours that penetrated into their camp of the national character of the insurrection, and its wide extent, unnerved the hearts of many. It was said that the Spanish colonists scattered among the plains and valleys had all been murdered ; that no relief could be brought up from the coast, because the Peruvians had possession of all the passes ; that siege had been laid to Lima and Trujillo and San Miguel, and that these and other places could not long hold out ; and, to pre-pare the Spaniards to give credence to these reports, eight or ten human heads were rolled into the *plaza*, by whose pallid features, though set fast in death, they recognized the countenances of some of their former brothers in arms.* Overcome by so painful a testimony to the success of the revolt, there were not a few who came to regard resistance as hopeless. Such, too, it seemed to the dauntless spirit of Hernando Pizarro, unless he could abate the fury of the attack. For this purpose, he selected some twenty of his bravest fighting men, and made a sortie along the Condesayo road. Wheeling round upon the Indians from that province, he charged them with so much vehemence that they fled in disorder to the rugged fastnesses of the sierra; but there they rallied again, reformed their ranks, and renewed the battle. Thence Hernando was recalled to the *plaza* by the increasing energy of the fight, which began to tell on the wearied Spaniards. The enemy allowed them no time to rest; their assaults still continued; and Vellacma, who commanded the fortress, never intermitted his showers of darts and stones and arrows. In the city, the Indians posted themselves upon the blackened walls of the desolate houses, and thence kept up the attack. So that neither by night nor day did the Spaniards dare to cease for a moment from their vigilance, so ceaseless was the battle, and so various the ways in which it was pressed. At one time they were compelled to destroy the barricades and fill up the pits with which the Indians sought to impede the progress of their cavalry; at another, to demolish the channels through which they were directing upon them the horrors of an inundation.

Thus for six days the struggle continued. The Indians

* A similar expedient was adopted by the Mexicans during the siege of Mexico.

were masters of nearly the whole of the city, and not a few of the Spaniards now advised that it should be abandoned, and that they should endeavour to cut their way through the invading ranks of the enemy, hazarding all upon one final effort. Then said Hernando, in cheerful tones, " I know not, Señors, why you wish to do this; for to my mind there is not, nor has there been, any cause of fear ;" and in the evening he summoned his captains and principal officers to receive a stern, cold reprimand. " I have called you together, gentlemen," he said, " because it appears to me that the Indians daily load us with greater disgrace, and I believe that this is due to the weakness of certain among us who openly preach that the city ought to be given up. But if you, Juan Pizarro, are of such an opinion, whence came your courage to defend it against Almagro, when he sought to rebel ? and as for you, Riquelme "—the treasurer—" it would seem to be a heinous thing for you to talk in this fashion, when you are charged with the custody of the King's fifths, and are compelled to give an account of them, with the same obligation as he has who is in charge of a fortress. And for you other Señors, who are Alcaldes and Regidors, to whom the execution of the law is committed in this city, it is not for you to commit so great a folly as to deliver it into the hands of these ' tyrants.'" He added, "It would be a pitiful thing to tell of me, Hernando Pizarro, that from any motive of fear he abandoned the territory which his brother, Don Francisco Pizarro, had conquered and colonized. Wherefore, gentlemen, in the service of God and the King, sustaining our houses and lands, let us die rather than desert them. If I am left alone, I will repay with my life the obligation which lies upon me, rather than have it said that another gained the city and that I lost it. Remember, that with vigour we may gain what appears impossible; and that without vigour even that which is easy becomes difficult."

To this vigorous appeal the Spaniards responded with renewed courage, and it was unanimously agreed that the defence should be continued so long as there was one stalwart arm to wield a sword. Then Hernando spoke out: "The men are weary and the horses exhausted; in our straitened condition it is impossible for us to hold the city two days longer, and it is imperative upon us to gain the fortress or to perish. Once the fortress is ours, the city is secure. To-morrow morning, therefore, I will take all the horsemen that remain, and capture that fortress." They answered, that the horsemen were ready to a man to die with him, or conquer. But Juan Pizarro, though suffering from a severe wound, interposed: "It was my fault that the fortress was not occupied, and I vowed that I would take it whenever it became necessary to do so. Ill would it seem, therefore, if, while I am alive, any other should undertake the duty for me."

The discussion ended in Hernando Pizarro giving way to his brother. Fifty men were selected to compose the forlorn hope, and Gonzalo, Pizarro, and a cavalier named Ponce de Leon, went as subordinate officers.

At dawn of day the gallant fifty were mounted and ready to start. Hernando, before they set out, instructed his brother on leaving the city to ride along the Inca's road,

L

from Cuzco to Los Reyes, for about a league, in order
to wheel round and gain the open ground immediately
beneath the fortress, where the action of the cavalry
would not be impeded by barricades or pit-falls. In the
meantime, he proceeded with the remainder of his little
force to attack a formidable work which the Indians had
erected with the view of preventing the Spaniards from
escaping to the plain. This work was held by twenty
thousand Indians from the province of Chinchasuqo, who,
when they saw the advance of the Spaniards, cried to one
another, " Those Christians with the good horses are
flying ; the others which remain are the sick.*   Let us
allow these to draw off, and then we can kill them all."
In the skirmish that ensued, the Indians did not evince,
perhaps for this reason, their usual desperate courage,
and Juan Pizarro and his fifty cleared the defence, and
hastened to fulfil their mission. Hernando retreated with
eager alacrity to the great square, to encounter another
immense body of Indians, who had penetrated thither
in his absence, and whom he charged with such determination that they took to flight.

Let us now follow Juan Pizarro. For three miles, as
directed, he rode along the Los Reyes road ; then,
wheeling to the right, he crossed the ridges until he
reached the open ground in front of the fortress, scattering the enemy before him as he advanced, and opening
up a communication between himself and his brother in

* " Aguelles Cristianes que ticum les cavalles buenos se van
huyendo, y estes que quedan son les dolientes."—VICENTE DE
VALVERD .

the city. Hernando thereupon despatched to his assistance the Spanish infantry and the Indian auxiliaries, with
a message warning him not to attack until nightfall, when
he might hope to surprise the enemy; and begging him
not to hazard his own person in the struggle. For his
wound prevented him from wearing his helmet, and to
enter the combat without that protection would be mad-
ness. Juan, however, disregarded his brother's advice in
both particulars. He threw the enemy off their guard by
making a pretence of bivouacking for the night; and
then sent his brother Gonzalo to carry some outworks in
front of the fortress These, however, proved to be so
strongly defended that he was compelled to hasten in
person to support the attack. Both brothers led the
charge with so undaunted a valour that it served as an
inspiration to their men, who seemed converted for the
nonce into paladins of romance, invulnerable and irresist-
ible; and forward they went with a rush that carried them
right up to the wall of the principal building. Encouraged
by this brilliant success, Juan Pizarro pushed his enterprise farther. · The entrance was an outwork projecting
from the body of the fortress ; on each side it was enclosed
by a low wall, but it was open at the top so that it might
be commanded from the battlements ; it had an outer
gate corresponding with the principal gate of the fortress.
Beneath this outwork the defenders had dug a deep pit-
fall, in which they hoped to entrap the Spanish horse;
but they were driven back in such numbers, and in such
confusion, by the impetuosity of the Spaniards, as to fill
up with their own bodies that which their own hands had

made. Across the bridge thus strangely provided poured the Christian warriors, with Juan Pizarro, like a true knight errant, leading them through the storm of arrows and javelins and stones ; but at this moment a stone crashed upon his unprotected head, and struck him to the ground. Still with cheerful voice he continued to direct and animate his men ; but the Indians came up in such masses to renew the defence that retreat was unavoidable, and the Spaniards, as they slowly fell back, carried their wounded leader with them. He survived but a fortnight, and died in great pain, though with all the courage of a Pizarro.*

On the following morning, Hernando reconnoitred the fortress, and came to the conclusion that, owing to the height of the wall, it could not be carried without scaling-ladders. As many hands as could be spared from the task of resisting the enemy were occupied all day in making them; while Gonzalo and Ponce de Leon struggled resolutely to maintain the forward position won by such strenuous energy. The Inca having reinforced the army with five thousand of his best troops, the attack was almost overwhelming; and we cannot but feel a combined surprise and admiration that a mere handful of Spaniards succeeded in repulsing it. By evening the scaling-ladders were finished, and while the horsemen protected their

* He was the most amiable and humane of the Pizarros, and the soldiers loved him dearly. Zarate says of him : " Fue gran pérdida en la tierra, porque era Juan Pizarro mui valiente, i experimentado en las guerras de los Indios i bien quisto, i amado de todos." This is no light praise. We may note here the strong brotherly affection which existed among the Pizarros, redeeming some of the darker features of their characters.

flanks, the foot soldiers hastened to the assault as fresh
and vigorous and eager as if the conflict had only just
begun, instead of having already lasted thirty hours. The
Indians were disheartened by this marvellous energy on
the part of their assailants, whom it seemed impossible to
weary or overcome. Moreover, their supplies of stones
and darts began to fail them, and Hernando saw with
pleasure that the defence was rapidly slackening. Villacma, the high priest, saw it also. He shrank before the
ardour of these unconquerable white men, and resolved
upon flight. With some of his more immediate followers
he stole out of the fortress, on the side which faced the
river, and by secret winding paths among the rocks and
precipices effected his escape, unknown to and unmolested by the Spaniards. He then withdrew his division,
the Chinchasayans, and hastened to report to the Inca
the capture of the fortress.

The capture, indeed, though not complete, could not
be long delayed. The walls were still guarded by a
brave Inca noble, and by a few heroic warriors, who, with
him, had pledged themselves to their royal master in the
golden cup, and were resolute to fulfil the pledge. He
was a man of stalwart thews and muscles, and strode to and
fro along the battlements, armed with a Spanish buckler
and cuirass, stripped from some dead enemy, and wielding
a heavy mace, studded with bosses or knobs of copper.
With this formidable weapon he struck down all who
ventured to oppose him. "There is not written," says
the chronicler, "there is not written of any Roman such
deeds as he did." It is said that with his own hand he

slew some of his countrymen who proposed a surrender. Had the Inca's army been wholly composed of men like him, the conquest of Peru would never have been accomplished by Pizarro. As each Spaniard who mounted the scaling-ladder gained the topmost round, he rushed upon him and hurled him to the ground beneath, for his strength was not inferior to his courage. Nor was his energy inferior to his strength; he was at every point most threatened with peril. Hernando, respecting his valour, gave orders that, if possible, he should be taken alive, and generously treated. But the chief, at last perceiving the defence was over, that his men were slain or exhausted, and that the Spaniards were swarming up their scaling-ladders all around the rampart, prepared to die. He hurled his mace down among his foes: in token of despair, he took some earth in his hands, bit it, and covered his head with it, in such anguish and heart-sickness as no words can describe. Then, wrapping his mantle around him, he threw himself headlong from the summit of the tower he had so valiantly defended, unwilling to endure the spectacle of the triumph of the enemy.*

The fortress was won; but the position of Hernando Pizarro's little force was still sufficiently perilous, and their leader knew that it would not be safe to relax ever

* The narratives of Pedro Pizarro and Vicente de Valverde differ considerably in their details of the siege. The former is closely followed by Prescott; the latter by Sir Arthur Helps. We have attempted to combine them in a consistent record, so that nothing of importance should be omitted.

HEROIC DEFENCE OF CUZCO.

so little in his activity until he had more effectually
secured it. While his followers were still elated with
their triumph, he led them against the Chinchasayan
Indians, and the onset was made with so much vehemence
that they were thrown into the most extreme confusion,
and fled, leaving the ground covered with dead bodies.
On the following day he was not less successful in an
attack upon the Collasayans; and on the third day he
assailed and defeated the Condesayans; so that he had
cleared the plain of his enemies, and opened up a communication with the surrounding country. Even then
he did not rest. He was not blind to the possibility
that he and his little force might be the only Spaniards
left in all Peru, or, at least, that Lima might have been
besieged at the same time as Cuzco; that, consequently,
the Marquis could not forward any reinforcements, and
that therefore their trust must be put in their own good
swords. It was true that Almagro and a well-equipped
army were in Chili, but Hernando knew that his feelings
towards the brothers of Pizarro were the reverse of
friendly. No; he must be his own resource; or, as he
told his men, they must make their hearts broad enough
to bear whatever burden might be put upon them.
"Since God had been pleased," he said, "to give them
the glorious victory by which they had gained the fortress,
and saved the city from a state of siege, he was of opinion
that, in order to secure the enjoyment henceforward of
some rest and peace, and to strengthen their hold on
the city, they ought to collect supplies of provisions from
the valley of Sacsahuana. For if they did not seize upon

the maize growing there, the Indians might anticipate them, and they would then have to obtain their supplies from a distance." His soldiers listened with grim faces to this appeal, for they were battle-worn and in need of rest; but they obeyed, like true men, and with a sufficient following Gonzalo set out for the fertile valley. In five days he returned, followed by a long train of Indian men and women, laden with the precious maize.

The siege, which the Peruvians had interrupted in order to celebrate their usual New Moon ceremonies, now recommenced, and the prudence of Hernando Pizarro's policy became apparent, inasmuch as it enabled the Spaniards to maintain the defence with vigour. For twenty days the Indians persisted in their attacks, and then again desisted to offer their usual monthly sacrifices. Hernando Pizarro took advantage of this new respite to assume the offensive, and he attacked the Indians in their encampments with great success and cruel slaughter. But for a third time the hosts of the enemy closed round Cuzco, and the Spanish commander determined on a singular but terrible scheme. Humane as he had always shown himself in his treatment of the natives, and humane as certainly was his natural disposition, necessity forced upon him a resolve worthy of an Attila. He ordered his men, in their pursuit of the enemy, to kill all the Indian women they fell in with, so as to deter the sur-vivors from coming to serve their sons and husbands.*

* "Hernando Pizarro . . , mando á todos los Españoles que en los alcances dexasen mugor á vida porque colerando miedo las que quedason libres, no vendrian á servir á suo marides y hijos."— VICENTE DE VALVERD

This sanguinary but sagacious device had all the success which its author anticipated; and the Indians eventually abandoned the si :ge, husbands fearing to lose their wives and sons their mothers, while the women dreaded the merciless swords of the Spaniards.

Hernando, with characteristic vigour, immediately undertook the offensive. He gave his men no rest, but day after day, in one direction or another, led them against the Indians, as if bent on a war of extermination. On one occasion, having defeated a body of Indians, he found among the spoil a couple of packages; and on opening them, discovered in one the grisly burden of six heads of Spaniards, and in the other numerous tattered letters. From these he ascertained that the Marquis had sent reinforcements from Lima to Cuzco, and as none had arrived, he could not do otherwise than conclude that they had been cut off. To confirm his suspicions, he put some of his prisoners to the torture, and wrung from them the information that the various parties of Spaniards despatched from Lima had all been severally surrounded and slain, so that the Inca could boast as trophies two hundred heads of Christian warriors, and one hundred and fifty skins of horses. The poor wretches in their agony also declared that the Spaniards had embarked from Los Reyes, and quitted the country. This was not true, though the Marquis had been in such peril that the Indians may possibly have believed that he could have had no other resource.

That such tidings should involve the small Spanish garrison of Cuzco in profound depression might well be expected. Hernando Pizarro, however, did not lose heart, and he hastened to revive the spirits of his followers. "Noble and very valorous gentlemen," he said, "I am greatly surprised, and not without reason, that you who so greatly esteem honour should show any sign of weakness at a time when you have need for the utmost fortitude. Now is the time, when Indian affairs are doubtful, to show your desire to gain distinction in the service of your Prince. If the bad news we have heard be true in every particular, which may not be the case, remember that your dead comrades have fallen in God's service, and in the defence of these kingdoms. That the Governor has departed is a thing for which we should be glad, inasmuch as it leaves more glory for us Deeply as I am indebted to my illustrious brother, I am not sorry that he will have no share in the victory which I intend to win ; that is, in the retention of these provinces. We have ample provisions to maintain us for a year and a half: we will sow more grain in the proper season, and then we shall be able to hold this city for six years. Right well pleased shall I be if, in all that time, no succour comes from beyond the seas, so that we may suffice in ourselves alone."

In pursuance of his brave resolve, Hernando renewed his expeditions against the Indians, displaying, in their conduct, the highest skill and most splendid courage. In one of them, having captured a large number of Indians and carried them into Cuzco, he adopted the cruel expedient of cutting off the right hands of four hundred, and sending the mutilated wretches to the

Inca. The Indians were so dismayed by this evidence of his relentless courage, that they withdrew all their forces from those districts, and the Spaniards, accordingly, were less severely harassed. Yet each month, after their usual religious festivals, the Indians renewed their attacks; and as it was Hernando Pizarro's policy always to despatch an expedition when the Indians retired on these occasions, it fell out that, during that year of the war, not for a single day did the whole Spanish garrison rest. As fast as one company returned from its raid, another company issued forth to carry fire and sword into some other quarter.

Prescott remarks that these contests were not confined to large bodies of troops (on the Spanish side "large bodies" could not possibly be collected!), but skirmishes took place between smaller parties, which sometimes assumed the form of personal combat. Nor were the combatants always unequally matched; the Peruvian warrior, with sling, bow, and lasso, often proved no contemptible antagonist for the mailed horseman, whom he sometimes even ventured to encounter, hand to hand, with his formidable battle-axe. "The ground around Cuzco became a battle-field, like the *vega* of Granada, in which Christian and pagan displayed the characteristics of their peculiar warfare; and many a deed of heroism was performed, which wanted only the song of the minstrel to shed around it a glory like that which rested on the last days of the Moslem in Spain."

In one of his expeditions Hernando met with a reverse. With eighty picked horsemen, and a small body of veteran infantry, he had set out for a place called Tambo, in the hope of surprising and capturing the Inca, Manco. He reached Tambo unperceived and unopposed, but found the Peruvian position much stronger than he had expected. The lofty hill on which the palace-fortress stood was cut into steep terraces, each defended by a solid rampart of stone and sunburnt brick. Only on one side it sloped gradually towards the river Yucay; and there Hernando resolved to deliver his attack. Crossing the river, he took the fortress in the rear, and, under cover of the night, wound his way up the acclivity. But his approach had been observed; and, on his coming within bowshot, the wall was suddenly alive with dusky figures, among whom could be seen the Inca, directing the defence. The morning air rang with the Indian war-whoop, and a tremendous storm of all kinds of missiles clashed and clattered about the heads of the Spaniards. Incited by their leader, who had much of his brother's tenacity of purpose, they twice attempted to renew the assault; but the Indian's force was too overwhelming, and they were compelled to retreat sullenly, with clouds of Indians hanging upon their rear until they came within sight of the walls of Cuzco.

We must now glance for a moment at the position of affairs in Los Reyes, or Lima. As soon as the Marquis was apprised of the revolt of the Inca and the siege of Cuzco, he despatched to his brother's assistance a body of men under Gonzalo de Tapia; but they were intercepted by the insurgents and slain to a man. The same fate befell three other detachments and their leaders, so that the Spanish force in Peru was considerably weakened.

Some weeks elapsed before Pizarro became aware of these losses, and as no news arrived from Cuzco, he feared the worst. To maintain his hold upon Peru would be, he foresaw, a task of no little difficulty; and he sent an urgent summons to one of his most trusted lieutenants, Alonzo de Alvarado, whom he had ordered to conquer the province of Chacapeyas, to return to his assistance. He also implored the Governors of Panama, Nicaragua, Guatemala, and New Spain to forward reinforcements, that his fair conquest of Peru might not be lost to the crown of Castile. By this time a host of Indian fighting-men had swarmed around Los Reyes; it was estimated that they numbered fully fifty thousand, under the command of a great Inca noble, Teyyupangui. At first the Marquis decided to go out and attack them; but on further reflection he deemed the risk too great, and resolved to await the onset behind the recent ramparts of Los Reyes.

Teyyupangui had pledged himself to the Inca to capture the city or perish in the effort. He addressed his men in martial language, appealing to their patriotic pride and religious feelings. He designed, he said, to force his way that day into the Spanish city, and to kill all the Spanish inhabitants. Then they would take their wives, marry them, and have children by them fitted for war. But none, he added, were to accompany him who would not swear that if he died they should all die, and if he fled they all should flee. There were none among his captains who refused this pledge; and with a great pageantry of banners, the army moved forward to the attack. Their immense numbers poured over the walls and into the streets, Teyyupangui marching in front, with his spear in his hand. But as soon as they were on level ground, the Spanish horsemen effected a brilliant charge, which carried them through the Indian ranks like a hurricane through a grove of palms. Their track was shown by a long line of the dead and dying, who included Teyyupangui and his captains. The Indians fell back, disheartened; the Spaniards repeated their charge, and soon the plain was dark with the flying companies of the broken army. Next day they retired into the mountains, and Los Reyes was out of danger.

Shortly after this great victory, Alonzo de Alvarado arrived, and the Marquis was able to despatch him, with one hundred horsemen and one hundred and fifty foot-soldiers, to chastise the Indian insurgents in the province of Xauxa, but not to advance unto the relief or recapture of Cuzco until he had been reinforced. This was in the month of October. Scattering the Indians before him Alvarado arrived at Xauxa, where he waited for four months, according to the Marquis's instructions.

Again the scene changes, and we must follow in the track of Almagro the Mariscal, whom we last saw at the head of an expedition destined for the conquest of Chili. Along the great road of the Incas he marched until he reached the Chilian frontier; after which he plunged into the pathless defiles of the Cordilleras, and with pain and labour continued his progress southward. To the eye of the artist the scenery of the Andes is a succession

of grand and imposing effects ; great torrents roll down
the rugged declivities, and in vast shining cataracts
tumble into seemingly fathomless abysses ; dense forests
of pine climb up the sides of the ravines, and fill the
echoes with a mighty rushing sound ; broad spaces
of tableland, without tree or shrub, seem the chosen
battlefields of contending winds ; and far up into the
deep blue sky, higher than even the condor's wing can
soar, rise the white forms of the mountain-peaks.   But
to the leader of armed men all this is a weariness and
a snare ; he knows that each feature of sublimity will
involve him in some loss of life.   Almagro's followers
had worse enemies to struggle with than the Indians ;
their continual foes were the intense cold, which chilled
their blood and benumbed their limbs, and famine, which
paralyzed their energies and depressed their spirits.   The
Spaniards were forced to feed on the frozen carcasses of
their horses ; their Indian attendants and followers, less
fortunate, on the dead bodies of their countrymen.
Happy, therefore, was their commander when he emerged
upon the warm and fertile valley-plain of Coquimbo,
where he and his soldiers could enjoy unbounded plenty
and secure repose.

When he had recruited the energies of his men, he
sent an officer forw rd, with a small force, to reconnoitre
the country towards the south.   Meantime, the remainder
of his little army arrived, under the bold fierce soldier
Rodrigo de Orgoñez, who brought with him the royal
warrant conferring on Almagro the governorship of all
lands conquered south of Peru.   It was immediately

argued by Almagro's intimates that Cuzco must lie within the limits of his territory, and they strenuously urged him to retrace his steps and reclaim from Pizarro that golden city. In this they were supported by Almagro's soldiers, who were already weary of a region which seemed bare of gold and silver, and held out no promise of either profit or pleasure. When the recon- noitring party returned with the information that, after a march of one hundred and fifty leagues, they had lighted upon no rich settlements, no populous and wealthy towns, no temples and palaces blazing with gold or gems, the clamour in the camp redoubled, and Almagro, who had never a firm command over his men, was fain to yield to it. Abandoning his designs upon Chili, he wheeled round his army, and prepared to march back upon Cuzco,—to which, it is clear, he had neither a legal nor a moral claim. Shrinking from a fresh experience of the mountain route, he took his way along the coast, which compelled him to traverse the great desert of Atacama. In avoiding Scylla, he had fallen into Charybdis. The desert proved as inhospitable as the mountains; it demanded, like the mountains, its toll of dead from the rash adventurers who had pro- faned its solitudes! But the wonderful hardihood and astonishing energy of the Spaniards carried them through every trial, and they reached at length the picturesque town of Arequipa. Here, at a distance of sixty leagues from Cuzco, he learned that the Peruvians had risen against the invaders, and that the young Inca, with a still formidable army, lay between him and the capital.

At the same time the news of his approach was carried
to Hernando Pizarro, who could not doubt, from the very
fact of the Mariscal's return, that he came as an enemy.

Almagro, however, did not at once march upon Cuzco.
He arranged, through his emissaries, a meeting with
the Inca in the valley of Yucay, and with half his force,
or about two hundred and forty men, proceeded to the
rendezvous, while he ordered the other half to take up
their quarters at Urcos, about twenty miles from Cuzco.
Hernando at the same time issued from the capital, and
encamped with his small force in the vicinity. The
Peruvians, observing the proximity of the two camps,
not unnaturally concluded that they understood each
other, and that Almagro's negotiation with the Inca was
a subtly-devised plot to get possession of his person.
They made a sudden assault, therefore, with fifteen
thousand men, on the Spaniards in the valley of Yucay;
but these veterans had kept a vigilant outlook, and were
prepared for the shock. The Inca's army was driven
back with great slaughter, and Almagro then hastened to
concentrate his forces at Urcos. Thereupon he sent an
embassy to its municipality, presenting a copy of his
credentials from the Crown, and requiring them to recog-
nise him as their governor. The authorities professed
themselves unable to decide between the rival claimants,*
and asked for time to investigate the question. A truce
was accordingly arranged between the contending parties

---

* Cuzco, however, was unquestionably within the limits of
Pizarro's jurisdiction, which, indeed, extended half a degree further
south.

of which Pizarro availed himself to open up negotiations with Almagro. He insisted on the importance of peace being preserved between them, as, otherwise, all would be lost, and the Inca would recover his supremacy over the country. He offered to receive him in the city with all honour, and intimated that his quarters had been sui'ably prepared for his accommodation. And more particularly did he urge that a messenger should be despatched to the Marquis in order that he might come and settle matters without bloodshed.

Almagro returned an evasive answer, and on Monday, the 18th of April, 1537, moved forward to a position within three leagues of the city. Hernando Pizarro once more invited him to enter it as a friend. "Tell him," was the reply, "that I will not enter the city except as my own, nor lodge in any lodgings but those where he is,—that is, in the Governor's apartments." Yet again did Hernando Pizarro attempt to bring about an arrangement, enlarging on the perils that might arise from further action on the part of the Indians, and soliciting Almagro to preserve the peace until the Marquis should arrive. Almagro, who seems to have been greatly influenced by his lieutenant, Orgoñez, replied that he held his government from the Emperor, and was determined to enter his own capital. And, raising his tents, he moved forward within a bowshot of the city. Hernando still desired to avoid hostilities; and calling a meeting of the Council, he obtained their consent to his proposal that an Alcalde, accompanied by two Regidors, should repair to Almagro, and, in the Emperor's name, require

of him that he should not disturb the city, but that if
he possessed powers from his Majesty, should present
them before the Council, in order that they might judge
of their extent.   To so moderate a request Almagro
could not return a refusal, and accordingly a truce was
proclaimed for twenty-four hours. On the fo'lowing morning he laid his powers before the Council (Hernando, at his
request, having been excluded), who, after due consideration, decided that they were ready to obey the Emperor's
orders ; and that, as his Majesty had allotted to Almagro
for territory two hundred leagues reckoning from the
boundary-line of Don Francisco Pizarro's, and as the
said territory had not been set out or defined, and as
Don Francisco Pizarro had occupied Cuzco as within
his government, the division-line of the two governments
should be carefully ascertained by " pilots " or experts ;
and that, until this had been done, Almagro should
refrain from forcing an entrance into the city, and bringing ruin upon both parties.   When the division was
settled, if Cuzco proved to be within Almagro's jurisdiction, they would loyally accept him as Governor.

In a storm of rage Almagro ordered his soldiers to
prepare to attack the city, and Hernando immediately
summoned his men to the defence.   But another effort
was made by the loyal Treasurer and a licentiate named
Prado, to avoid armed collision; and their entreaties
induced Almagro to extend the truce until the hour of
Vespers next day (Wednesday).

The weather was severe, and the snow lay on the
ground.   The soldiers longed for the shelter and con-

venient accommodation of the city; and there were
rumours abroad that Alvarado, with a large body of men,
was marching to the assistance of Hernando Pizarro.
Of these circumstances Orgoñez and others availed themselves to persuade Almagro into an immediate attack.
They commented on the unfavourable character of their
position, and pointed out that while every day might
increase Pizarro's strength, every day would diminish
Almagro's. To his eternal dishonour, Almagro, in whose
character there was a fatal element of weakness, yielded
to this counsel, and at midnight suddenly pushed
forward his soldiers into the great square. Orgoñez,
with a large body of infantry, hastened to surround the
dwelling of Hernando, who, with his brother Gonzalo,
was lodged in one of the large public halls built by the
Emperor. Hernando Pizarro was in bed when the alarm
was given; but he sprang up has il , donned his armour,
and prepared to make a stout defence. About twenty
soldiers stood by him, and for some time the assailants
made but little progress. Blood was shed on both sides,
when Orgoñez, enraged at the gallant resistance, seized
a torch, and set fire to the thatched roof of the hall.
The flames spread rapidly, and as the burning timbers
fell in upon the brave little garrison, the two Pizarros
were compelled to surrender. They were thrown into
captivity in the House of the Sun, and put in chains.

Almagro began to govern Cuzco with a high hand,
and to bear with a sharp pressure on the members of the
Pizarro faction. Presuming on his new position, he sent
envoys to Alonzo de Alvarado's camp, requiring him to

recognize him as legitimate master of the city. In reply, Alvarado, who had received reinforcements from the Marquis, and was at the head of two hundred cavalry and five hundred foot, put the envoys in irons, and sent to Los Reyes for instructions.* Almagro, in the interval, had made another effort to negotiate with Manco, but failing, he invested Manco's brother, Paullo, with the *borla*, and thus obtained the services of some ten thousand Indian auxiliaries. With those, and his Spanish soldiers, he moved against Alvarado. His lieutenant, Orgoñez, recommended him before his departure to behead the Pizarros, declaring that while they lived his life would never be safe ; and adding, in the words of an old proverb, " Dead men never bite."† The Mariscal was ill affected towards Hernando, but he hesitated at such a deed of murderous violence. Moreover, apart from all political considerations, he was unwilling to put a sea of blood between himself and his old associate the Marquis, the influence of their long friendship not having wholly decayed. He contented himself, therefore, with placing a strong guard over his prisoners before he quitted the city. He was encouraged in his design by the treachery of Pedro de Lerma, one of Alvarado's principal officers, who had secretly entered into communication

---

* The Marquis, on receiving the information brought by Alvarado's horsemen, sent him strict orders not to move on Cuzco : but, unfortunately, his messengers did not leave Los Reyes in time to prevent the march.

† " El muerto no mordia."—HERRERA, " Hist. General," dec. vi., lib. ii., c. 8.

with him, and promised to join him in person, and to bring several partisans. This man informed him of all the particulars of Alvarado's movement, and of the position he had taken up at the Bridge of Abançay.*

* See the account in Garcilasso de la Vega's "Commentarios Reales" (2nd pt.), lib. ii., c. 34.

CHAPTER VI.

THE FEUD BETWEEN ALMAGRO AND PIZARRO.—
EXECUTION OF ALMAGRO.

LVARADO had posted his men on the further bank of the Rio de Abançay, opposite the bridge, while a ford lower down was guarded by a detachment. At nightfall Almagro ordered his artillery to open fire, and his Indians to keep up a continual shouting and discharge of missiles, so as to delude the enemy into a belief that he intended to force the passage of the bridge; while through the darkness he led three hundred horsemen to the ford, and there, with the guidance of Pedro de Lerma's men crossed unopposed, but not without losing some of his troopers in the rapid current. Immediately he attacked the detachment on the river-bank, who had been misled by the traitors, put them to the rout, and advanced towards the bridge. By this time the alarm had been given, and Alvarado, with about fifty men, was hastening to support the guard at the ford, when he encountered Almagro's soldiers—who, on account of the roughness of the ground, had dismounted—in the narrow belt of ground lying between the sierra and the river. Here a gallant fight took place, in which the Almagrists got the worst. Perceiving this, they cried to one another, "To the hills! Let us gain the hills!" But Alvarado saw that if they occupied the hills they could cut him off from his camp and intercept his communications with Pizarro; wherefore, followed by a few of his veterans, he climbed the heights with all speed. Almagro's men, however, not less swift-footed than himself, reached the summit as quickly; so that Alvarado found himself hopelessly outnumbered, and unable to prolong the contest. A prisoner, he was carried down to the bridge, which Almagro's infantry had successfully forced, and there was no alternative but for all his little army to surrender (July 12th).

Orgoñez, always athirst for blood, advised the execution of Alvarado, but Almagro would not consent; and on the 14th of July he marched back to Cuzco in triumph, with a long array of prisoners. Here his successes did not end; for his lieutenant, Orgoñez, soon afterwards defeated the Inca's army, and very nearly captured the Inca himself; and his brain dizzying with his triumphs, he began to think of claiming even Los Reyes as within the boundaries of his government.* Such an exaltation of spirit is often observed in men who have risen to power and prosperity just before their fall. But Almagro must have been strangely ignorant of the tenacity and reso-

* His troops partook of their leader's arrogance, and were heard to say that they would not leave one *Pizarra* (*i.e.*, a "a slate") to stumble over.

lution of his great rival, who now, after a long interval of comparative inaction, reappears on the scene.

Francisco Pizarro had waited with calm patience for the reinforcements which alone could enabie him to strike a decisive blow. Slowly they arrived; and among them, at last, came his old associate, the Licentiate Gaspar de Espiñosa, with two hundred and fifty horse and foot. He also received from Cortes, the great Mexican conqueror, a vessel laden with supplies and provisions, and, as a special token of friendship, a costly wardrobe for himself.

With a force amounting to four hundred and fifty men, about equally divided into horse and foot, the Marquis quitted Lima and began his march upon Cuzco. He had advanced but a few leagues, when he received the astounding intelligence of Almagro's abandonment of his expedition to Chili, the seizure of Cuzco, the imprisonment of his brothers, and the defeat at Abançay. These reverses did not shake his indomitable courage; but apprehending that Almagro's success might embolden him to attack Lima, he returned in all haste to the capital to strengthen and complete its defences. He felt very keenly the injustice with which he had been treated by his comrade of many years ; personal feelings, however, never affected Pizarro's line of policy, and he determined, before drawing the sword, to extend "the olive branch" of peace to his powerful rival. For this purpose he sent to him an embassy, consisting cf Gaspar de Espiñosa, the Licentiate de la Gama, the Factor Suarez de Carvajal, and Diego de Fuenmaya, men of position and moderation, in whose discretion both parties might fairly trust. They repaired to Cuzco; but Almagro, either under the influence of Orgoñez, or inflated by his unaccustomed authority, would listen to no terms of accommodation. He insisted not only upon the possession of Cuzco, but upon that of Los Reyes. In vain Gaspar de Espiñosa pointed out the futility of his pretensions; Almagro declared he would maintain them with his sword. In vain the Licentiate enlarged on the injury to the interests of the Crown, which must result from a collision between the Marquis and himself. In vain he argued that the American continent afforded ample scope for the exercise of his ambition, without his entering upon a course of action, for the sake of a few leagues more or less, which would offend high Heaven, irritate the King, and fill the world with scandal and disaster. Almagro would make no concession, would hear of no compromise. The Licentiate turned angrily on his heel: "Soon will you learn," he exclaimed, "the force of the old proverb, 'The conquered conquered, and the conqueror undone.'"*

Soon afterwards the negotiations came to an abrupt close, through the sudden death of Espiñosa, which was attributed, however, entirely to natural causes. The influence of his cool judgment and sagacity removed, there was no longer any barrier to the violence of both factions. Carrying Hernando Pizarro with him,—for he feared his daring character and fertility of resource,—and

* "El vencido vencido. y el vencidor perdido."

leaving in prison at Cuzco his brother Gonzalo, and Alonzo de Alvarado, Almagro at once began his move-ment upon Los Reyes. He had got no further than the valley of Lanasca, when messengers rode after him with the intelligence that Gonzalo Pizarro and Alvarado had bribed their guards, and effected their escape. Orgoñez immediately advised him to put Hernando to death : "A Pizarro," he said, " was never known to forget an injury ; and that which they have already received from you is too deep to be forgiven." But Almagro seems still to have cherished some vague hope of an accommodation with the Marquis, and hesitated to commit a crime which must have rendered it impossible. He was confirmed in this disposition by the influence of Diego de Alvarado, of whom, in his calmer moods, he frequently took counsel. Diego was a gallant, an accomplished, and a generous cavalier. He had had friendly relations with Hernando, and strongly protested against his execution. " It would not only," he said, " influence to the utmost the passions of the Pizarrists, but would provoke the indignation of the Court of Castile." Almagro listened to his milder words, and spared Hernando. No doubt, as a matter of policy, Orgoñez was right. Almagro had gone too far to recede, and his safety lay in going farther. When a man once enters on a course of violence, it becomes equally impossible for him to go back or to stand still ; the accumulating impetus of his violent actions hurries him onward fatally, and whether he attempts to arrest his progress, or whether he yields to the power behind him, ensures, sooner or later, his destruction. It was probable that a reconciliation might be effected with the Marquis; old associations and motives of policy might incline him to a peaceful settlement; but Almagro should have known that Hernando Pizarro would never forget the indignity that had been put upon him.

Towards the end of August, Almagro reached the vale of Chincha, where, in imitation of Pizarro, he laid the foundation of a town to which he gave his own name. By this time the resources of his rival had wonderfully increased; reinforcements had arrived from all quarters, and he had had the pleasure of welcoming the fugitives from Cuzco; so that he found himself at the head of one thousand men-at-arms, of whom not the least formidable was a contingent of one hundred and fifty well-equipped arquebusiers. He felt strong enough to make a final effort at negotiation; and after a prolonged correspondence between Almagro and himself, it was agreed that their dispute should be referred to an arbiter, and that this arbiter, with the assistance of "pilots," should fix the boundaries of their respective territories. The arbiter chosen was the Provincial Fray Francisco de Bobadilla, of the Order of Mercy. Needless to say that the fiery Orgoñez objected strongly to both the arbitration and the arbiter! His objections, however, were set aside; and Bobadilla and his "pilots" repaired to an Indian town called Mala, which was situated about midway between Los Reyes and Chincha, and there summoned each Governor to appear before him, attended by twelve horsemen only.

Pizarro and Almagro hastened to obey; but so much

had occurred to shake the confidence of the Pizarrists, that they induced Gonzalo Pizarro, unknown to the Marquis, to move the army forward in the direction of Mala. The two great captains met in the presence of Bobadilla on the 13th of November. There is a difference in the accounts of the method of their meeting: one authority representing it as very friendly, so that they shed tears and exchanged affectionate greetings; another declaring that Pizarro assumed his haughtiest demeanour when Almagro, doffing his bonnet, advanced "in his usual open manner," to salute his ancient comrade. We have little doubt that the former statement is true; and it seems that the two Governors were on the point of coming to an amicable understanding, when an unfortunate incident—one of those mysterious "chances" which so often in life break up the subtlest schemes and baffle the most assured hopes—changed the entire current of their destiny. It is said that Francisco de Godey, one of Gonzalo's captains, apprised the Almagrists of the danger impending over them by singing a couplet of an old ballad—

> " Tiempo es el caballero,
> Tiempo es de andar de aqui ;"

and that therefore an Almagrist, named Juan de Gayneau, hastily entered the apartment where the Governors were in conference, and whispered in Almagro's ear that he was the dupe of some intended treachery. Without a word of farewell or explanation, the Mariscal turned his back on his rival, strode down the stairs, mounted a horse which Juan de Gayneau had brought for him, and rode rapidly away.

This unexpected occurrence proved to be the turning-point of the fortunes of both Almagro and Pizarro. In vain the Marquis sent word next day that the advance of his army had been without his knowledge or permission, and begged Almagro to return and complete their inchoate arrangement. He rejected every advance, and wrapped himself in a cloak of secrecy and suspicion. Without further reference to either party, the arbiter then pronounced his award, which was entirely in Pizarro's favour, and, indeed, it is impossible for the impartial historian to see how it could have been otherwise. He declared that Cuzco lay within the two hundred and seventy-five leagues which the Emperor had defined as the limit of Pizarro's territory, and must therefore be surrendered to him; and, at the same time, he decided that Hernando Pizarro should be released on condition that, within six weeks, he left the country for Spain. Both parties were to retire within their respective territories, and lay down the sword.

The Almagrists broke out into a frenzy of rage when this award became known to them. They denounced it as unjust, and calumniated the arbiter as a hireling of Pizarro's, while Orgoñez renewed his demand for Hernando Pizarro's head. Almagro himself protested that he should disregard the arbiter's decision. But wiser counsels prevailed. The good influence of Diego de Alvarado was brought to bear on the impetuous temper of his aged leader, while the Marquis, anxious for the life of his brother, and the preservation of Spanish interests in

Peru, was fully prepared to make any reasonable concessions. The arrangement finally effected was as follows : That Chincha should be evacuated ; that Cuzco
should, so to speak, be neutralised until the King's
decision as to its ownership could be obtained ; that
Almagro should prosecute his conquests southward, and
Pizarro northward ; that Hernando Pizarro should be
liberated on condition that he left the country in six
weeks; and that Pizarro should place one of his ships at
Almagro's disposal. When these terms were made known
to Orgoñez, that truculent cavalier gave way to a storm
of passion. " Never," he said, " were the perfidious in
want of excuses for not fulfilling their promises ! " And,
lifting up his beard with his left hand, he drew his right
across his throat with a significant gesture, exclaiming :
" Orgoñez, Orgoñez, this is what thy fidelity to thy master
will cost thee ! "

Almagro, however, adhered to the conditions of his
pact. He repaired in person to Hernando Pizarro's place
of confinement, and made known to him that he was at
liberty, embracing him with much fervour, and expressing
a hope that "all past feuds would be forgotten, and that
thenceforward peace and good-fellowship might prevail."
Hernando replied that it would not be his fault if it were
not so, for he desired nothing better ; and he swore by
his honour as a knight that he would faithfully fulfil the
stipulations of the treaty. The Mariscal then conducted
him to his quarters, and entertained him right hospitably,
together with his principal officers, some of whom afterwards escorted him half way to his brother's camp

Almagro's son, Don Diego, and the Alvarados rode with him all the way, and were courteously received by the Marquis, who bestowed upon them many gifts, and in particular lavished his attentions on the young Diego. Thus it seemed to the ordinary observer as if the storm had completely passed over ; the air was clear, the angry voices of the battling winds were hushed. But those whose eyes were keener did not fail to see that threatening clouds still hung upon the distant horizon.

On the day of Hernando's release arrived an envoy from the Court of Spain, one Pedro de Ançurez, bearing important despatches. Important indeed, for they re-opened the quarrel which seemed to have been satisfactorily composed, by providing that each governor should hold the territory he had conquered and settled ("conquistado y pobludo ") until the Emperor made some other arrangement. The Marquis immediately accepted this decision as fatal to Almagro's pretensions; nor could there be any doubt that Cuzco was within his conquests, and that Los Reyes had been founded by himself. To Almagro, therefore, who had retired to the valley of Zangala, and was bent on colonizing it, he intimated that their treaty was at an end, and that he must abandon all further claim to Cuzco, which the imperial decision had now definitely made over to the Marquis's government. At the same time he forbade the departure of Hernando to Spain, and released him from his engagements to Almagro, as engagements that could not apply when the conditions were wholly altered. Hernando, however, submitted reluctantly, feeling that he had pledged his knightly honour, and fearing the imputations that the Almagrists would throw upon his good faith. But he did not refuse to take the command of his brother's army, which advanced as far as Chincha.

Some time was wasted in the mutual recriminations of the two parties, but on the close approach of the Pizarros, Almagro withdrew to Guaytara, a mountain pass which offered an almost impregnable strategical position. Pizarro's soldiers followed, a·ter lis·ening to an animated address from Hernando. "To all of you," he said, "the bounty shown by the Emperor to the Governor, my brother, is fully known ; and though, before this imperial mandate arrived, the justice on our side was manifest, his Majesty's new confirmation of it gives us still greater certainty. On our side, then, I repeat, we have justice ; on Almagro's there is greed. You are now about to show your fidelity to my brother, but also your loyalty to the Crown; and if you replace this province under the imperial authority, doubt not that a liberal reward will await your services. I know well," he continued, "that I do greatly err, when there are so many cavaliers and soldiers zealous in the cause of their prince, to insist on their obligation to serve him, inasmuch as I cannot magnify it so much as to make it equal to your desire to show it by your deeds. Therefore, in that conviction, I will leave to the future the demonstration and proof of your loyalty, and your sense of the justice of our cause. But if any among you be in need of arms or horses, I pray you tell me, and I will cause him to be provided according to his wants; for as many of you, noble gentlemen and

N

cavaliers, have come from afar, you may be deficient in some things."

Encouraged and satisfied by this generous speech, the Pizarrists moved cheerfully forward, though Almagro refused to believe that they would attack an almost impregnable position, which was defended by a large body of Indian auxiliaries as well as by a division of his own troops. The rest of his army was entrenched in the rear at Guaytara. Hernando, however, observed that the heights above the pass were not very strongly guarded, their inaccessibility being considered a sufficient defence. To the brave and persevering nothing is impossible. In the evening twilight Hernando took with him three hundred men, and by a circuitous route rode to the foot of the sierra. Having dismounted, they began to climb the mountain—three miles of laborious ascent. A traitor in Pizarro's camp had revealed the design to Almagro's men, and they stood prepared to meet the rash intruder, though never believing that he would accomplish his enterprise. Through the darkness, however, he made his way, followed by his soldiers with patient alacrity. Early in the morning about five or six Pizarrists gained the summit, and raised a shout of " Viva el Rey!" with such vehement exultation that the Almagrists supposed the whole army to be upon them, and fled in confusion. It was midday, however, before the three hundred reached the summit. Almagro, thus taken in flank, had no alternative but to retreat. He was followed with more ardour than prudence by the Pizarrists, and the tide of war was nearly turned against them, Almagro having drawn up his forces in admirable order to stay their progress and crush their confused and breathless battalions. Hernando, with his soldier's eye, detecting the danger, advised an immediate retreat, and withdrew the army in safety to the valley of Ica, where the brothers remained for several weeks, refreshing and reorganizing their forces. Then the Marquis, who began to feel the weight of years, returned to Los Reyes, leaving Hernando to prosecute the campaign.

Almagro next turned his thoughts towards Cuzco, with the view of occupying it before the Pizarros could reach it. He was so enfeebled at this time by disease and old age that he was obliged to be carried in a litter ; and on reaching Bilcas his illness became so severe that he was detained for three weeks before he could resume his march. It was, therefore, the middle of April 1538, before he arrived in the vicinity of the capital of the Incas. With a sudden outburst of his old energy, he made vigorous preparations for holding it against the Pizarros. "In Cuzco," we are told, "nothing was heard but the sound of trumpets summoning to reviews, and the hammering of silver on the anvil, for of that metal it was that they made their corslets, cuirasses, and arm-pieces, which, using double the quantity of silver that they would have used of iron, they rendered as strong 'as if they had come from Milan.'" Nor were picks and spades idle, for earthworks were thrown up at every weak point of the defences. Provisions were also collected from all the country round ; scouts were posted on the high grounds to give notice of the approach of the enemy ; and the clang and murmur of

martial industry seemed to fill every echo, and were borne
on every wind.

Breaking up his camp at Ica, Hernando Pizarro ordered
a general advance. On reaching the valley of Lanasca,
he reviewed his men; and a goodly show they made in
their new equipments. They mustered in all six hundred
and fifty; of whom two hundred and eighty were horsemen, the remainder cross-bowmen, arquebusiers, and pike-
men. Well pleased with their appearance, and satisfied
of their fidelity, he advanced slowly and cautiously towards
Cuzco, in order to guard against a surprise. All marched
in full armour, so that they could give battle at any
moment. The journey was tedious, for the rivers were
swollen with the early thaws of spring, and to find a ford
it was often necessary to ascend high up their course.
Hernando insisted on the strictest discipline, and not a
few of his men deserted because he punished them for
robbing the natives. We have seen that Almagro had
resolved on defending the city; but on Hernando's approach, his commander, Orgoñez, changed his mind, and
confiding in his superior numbers, resolved to issue forth
from the city, and act on the offensive. So it came to
pass that when the Pizarrists reached an elevated plain,
south of Cuzco, called Las Salinas (or "the Salt Pits"),
they found Almagro's forces drawn out to oppose their
progress, with their front covered by a marsh and a small
stream, their flanks protected by horsemen and six small
cannon, or falconets. On the hill-side, near the Inca's
road, were posted the Indians, fifteen thousand strong,
under the Inca Paullo. Orgoñez himself was in com-

mand of the cavalry, who all wore white vests over their armour.

Slowly traversing the plain, the Pizarrists halted on the southern side of the little stream which trickled across the glittering plain. Here, as the sun was sinking, they took up their quarters for the night, purposing to come to blows with their enemies on the morrow. "The rumours of the approaching battle," says the historian,* "had spread far and wide over the country; and the mountains and rocky heights around were thronged with multitudes of natives, eager to feast their eyes on a spectacle where, whichever side were victorious, the defeat would fall on their enemies. The Castilian women and children, too, with still deeper anxiety, had thronged out from Cuzco to witness the deadly strife in which brethren and kindred were to contend for mastery. The whole number of the

* Prescott, ii., 103, 104. So, too, Sir Arthur Helps :—" We should judge but poorly of these combats in South America, if we estimated them according to the smallness of the number of men engaged on each side, and not according to the depth and amount of human emotion which they elicited. There was more passion in the two little armies now set over against each other, than is to be found in vast hosts of invading soldiers combating for objects which they scarcely understand. I have no doubt the hatred in these bands of Almagrists and Pizarrists greatly exceeded anything that was to be found in the ranks of the French and Spaniards that fought at Pavia. Even in religious wars, there has hardly existed greater fierceness than amongst these Spanish conquerors, where each man in the army was an aristocrat, fighting for lands, houses, slaves; and whose angry soul was often largely occupied by the remembrance of slights and injuries received from men in the opposite ranks, well known to him. It appears at first a slur upon the good sense of Her-nando Pizarro, and a sad inconsistency, that he, being a commander,

combatants was insignificant ; though not as compared with those usually engaged in these American wars. It is not, however, the number of the players, but the magnitude of the stake, that gives importance and interest to the game ; and on this bloody game they were to play for the possession of an empire. The night passed away in silence, unbroken by the vast assembly which covered the surrounding hill-tops. Nor did the soldiers of the hostile camps, although keeping watch within hearing of one another, and with the same blood flowing in their veins, attempt any communication. So deadly was the hate in their bosoms ! "

It was Saturday, the 26th day of April, 1538.

At early dawn, Hernando Pizarro assumed his surcoat of orange-damask, and donned his plumèd helm; not only that he might be known by his own men, but that he might easily be recognized by the enemy. As bold a warrior as he was a skilful leader, he intended to be

should give way to such feelings in his own case, while he strove to restrain the fury of others ; and his orange-damask surcoat and floating white feather seem but childish emblems in a general.* But the spirit of the times must not be forgotten. It was only in the preceding year that the outwardly sedate and almost always cautious Charles the Fifth, in the presence of the Pope and the College of Cardinals, had, after a passionate speech, prettily challenged the King of France to personal combat, staking Burgundy or Milan on the issue of the encounter. It is hardly to be wondered at, therefore, that Hernando Pizarro should give his personal enemies the means of knowing where he was to be found in the battle."—" History of the Spanish Conquest," iv., 101, 102.

---

* Hardly : when Henry of Navarre (" Henri Quatre of France ") wore a snow-white plume at the battle of Ivry that his soldiers might recognize him.

foremost in the fray, and to avenge upon some of the
Almagrists the contumely they had poured upon him
during his imprisonment. His trumpets having summoned his men to arms, he proceeded to array them ;
the infantry, which formed his chief strength, so large a
number being armed with arquebuses, in three companies in the centre, under Gonzalo Pizarro ; the horsemen, in two divisions, one on each flank, under Alonzo
de Alvarado and Pedro Ançurez. A small reserve was
placed under the command of a captain named Mercadillo. This order of battle having been formed, two
priests, splendidly robed, advanced to the front, and set
up two small altars, at which they chanted the mass and
gave the benediction. Pizarro then despatched a notary
to Almagro, formally requiring him to deliver up the city
of Cuzco ; and having discharged this useless ceremony,
he addressed some words of advice to his valiant soldiers.
He alluded briefly to the personal outrage his brother and
himself had undergone at Almagro's hands ; reminded
them that Cuzco had been unjustly wrested from the
Marquis's possession ; and pointed to it, as its towers and
walls shone in the morning sun, as the prize of their heroic
efforts. But it was not necessary, he said, to cheer or
encourage them ; rather did they need in their great
ardour to be restrained. He begged them to moderate,
with the patience that on such occasions was needful,
their desire for victory. They answered with a tremendous shout, and Hernando led them at once into
action. They waded the stream and struggled through a
marsh on the opposite side, their arquebusiers replying

with terrible effect to Almagro's artillery, and dealing death and wounds among his spearmen. Under cover of their steady fire, Hernando and his horsemen gallantly rode forward. Orgoñez, to oppose them, massed his squadrons together, and exclaiming: "O Divine Word, let those follow me who please, but I go to die," spurred against his antagonists. The shock was furious, but the Pizarrists bore it undauntedly, and the combatants were soon fighting hand to hand, cheering one another with their battle-cries of " El Rey y Almagro " and " El Rey y Pizarro," with which mingled the yells of Almagro's Indian auxiliaries from the height whence they looked forth upon the encounter.

However injudicious as a councillor, Orgoñez was a brave and chivalrous soldier, and in this, his last battle-field, his courage shone conspicuously. Mistaking a cavalier, from the colour of his surcoat, for Hernando Pizarro, he rode his horse at him full tilt, and bore him down with his lance. A second he slew in the same manner, and a third, who was shouting " Victory ! " he clave with his sword. In the heat of the *mêlée* he was smitten in the forehead by a chain-shot from an arquebus, which penetrated the bars of his visor, and momentarily stunned him. Before he had fully recovered himself, his horse was killed under him, and though he contrived to spring to the ground, he was quickly surrounded and overpowered. Looking round with a haughty glance, he said : " Is there no knight to whom I can surrender ? " One Fuentes, a menial of Pizarro, presented himself as if in answer to the question. Orgoñez delivered him his sword, whereupon the wretch drew his dagger and stabbed his defenceless prisoner to the heart. The head was struck off, stuck on a pike, and afterwards exhibited in the great square of Cuzco as the head of a traitor.

Not less eminent in the bloody strife was Hernando Pizarro ; his terrible lance seemed to carry everything before it, and his white plume shone above the clashing shields and swords and the waving helms like a meteor. Pedro de Lerma, the traitor, endeavouring to rally the Almagrist cavalry, made his way towards his enemy, and charged him with fell rancour ; but his lance, missing the rider, struck Hernando's horse, and bore it to its knees, whereas Hernando's spear transfixed the thigh of his opponent. In the fierce affray that followed Pedro de Lerma was unhorsed, and left on the field with many wounds. Hernando, on foot, defended himself with ready courage, until his soldiers swept around him, and rescued him from the increasing number of his enemies.

By his headlong charge, Orgoñez had uncovered the flank of his infantry, and Gonzalo Pizarro charged with complete success. The Almagrists gave way in great confusion, and took to flight with rapid feet, pursued by Gonzalo, who hunted them into the sierra. A few of Almagro's horsemen sought to prolong the contest, but one by one they were killed, wounded, or unhorsed, and those who survived were compelled to yield. Brought before Hernando Pizarro, he gave orders that their lives should be spared, thinking that the second victory which remained for him to win was a victory over himself, in repressing the dictates of private vengeance. Almagro, reclining in a litter, had watched the eddying fortunes of the two hours' fight, and on seeing it go against him, had succeeded in mounting a mule, and riding off to take shelter in the citadel of Cuzco. Thither he was followed by Alonzo de Alvarado, who carried him in triumph into the city, where he was thrown into irons, and (such are the strange contrasts of human life!) imprisoned in the same chamber of the palace in which he had imprisoned the two Pizarros. It is recorded that one of the Pizarrist captains, seeing the Mariscal for the first time, and scornfully observing his mean bearing and ill-favoured countenance, lifted his arquebus to kill him, exclaiming, " Is this the man for whom so many cavaliers have perished ? " But Alvarado struck up his arquebus, and forbade him to fire.

The battle of Las Salinas cost Almagro's party the lives of one hundred gallant soldiers. No account is given of the wounded, but their number could not have been less. Almost all the wounds were in the jaw; for the strong and complete armour of the Spaniards effectually protected every part of the body. The fortune of the day was decided in favour of the Pizarros, partly by Hernando's brilliant bravery and skilful conduct, but more by the heavy and deadly fire of his veteran arquebusiers, who had been trained in the Netherlands wars. It must be acknowledged that Pizarro used his victory leniently. We do not read of any executions or murders ; he treated his prisoners with courtesy, and he ordered that everything plundered on the day of battle should be restored to its owner. To gratify his lieutenants, and diminish the large number of soldiers of both parties assembled in Cuzco, he encouraged them to undertake the discovery and reduction of such provinces as had not hitherto submitted to the Spaniards. Alonzo de Alvarado set forth to conquer the Chacapoyas ; Pedro de Vergara to conquer the Beacamores ; and Mercadillo the district of Xauxa. Pedro de Candia was ordered on an expedition to the Andes, in which he was joined by many of the Almagrists ; who, however, when at a distance of about twenty leagues from the city, on the pretence of " re-organizing their ranks," entered into a nego- tiation with the captain of the arquebusiers, who had the custody of Almagro, to favour his escape, offering him 15,000 *castellanos* as a reward, and 1,000 *castel- lanos* for each of his men. The captain, however, reported the treacherous offer to Pizarro, who imme- diately arrested the traitors, and sent peremptory orders to Pedro de Candia to proceed on his expedition.

At the urgent solicitations of Almagro, Hernando Pizarro visited him in prison. He did his best to console the unfortunate captive, who gave way to inces- sant moans and tears ; reminding him that such reverses of fortune frequently occurred to valiant persons, and urging him to display the fortitude which alone was worthy of his greatness. He added an assurance that he should be kindly treated, and that if Pizarro did not speedily come to the capital, he would take it upon himself to release him and furnish him with the means of reaching his brother's quarters.

Hernando kept his word until he found that Almagro

was intriguing with Pizarro's officers, after which he was more closely confined and vigilantly guarded, while the King's officials instituted a formal process against him, and began to collect evidence.* This transaction occupied nearly four months, and Hernando Pizarro's object in it seems to have been to obtain justification for sending Almagro back to Spain. As a prisoner, the Mariscal must always be dangerous; if set at liberty, he would become the centre of new conspiracies; what, then, was to be done with him? The Almagrists, as it was, did not cease in their efforts to secure his release; and at last their plots compelled Hernando to take some decisive action.

Summoning a meeting of the municipal council, to which he invited his most experienced and sagacious officers, he laid before them the proofs he had obtained of a dangerous movement against the public peace. Already they knew, he said, the particulars of the troubles created by Don Diego de Almagro's men, and also by many of his own men, who, because he had compelled them to restore the booty they had taken in battle, and because of offers made on the Mariscal's part, had united with them. And now he had received the letter which he had placed in their hands, to the effect that Don Pedro de Candia had approached within nine leagues of the city, at the head of three hundred and fifty men, whose words showed that they came in a rebellious mood. They, the magistrates, were, like

* The evidence collected spread, we are told, over two thousand folio pages.

himself, responsible for the welfare of his Majesty's
service and the peace of the city; and as it was possible
that violent anger or prejudice might dispose him to do
something of which they would disapprove, he asked
them to look at the position of affairs, at the danger
which might occur, and the punishment there might be
for it; and, as men of honour and good judgment,
advise him what course to adopt, so that his Majesty
might be served and the peace of the city maintained.
And as it might be that some of them would not deliver
their opinions with perfect freedom in his presence, he
would retire from the council. He entreated them
carefully to consider what advice they gave, for only
upon that advice would he act; rather would he err in
following the common opinion, than succeed by following his own. Very fair and impartial this, no doubt;
but it must be remembered that Hernando was addressing the nominees of his brother, and the captains in his
brother's army, all of whom had nothing to gain from
Almagro and much to lose from Pizarro.

After a decorous interval, Hernando was invited to
hear the decision of the council. We shrewdly suspect
that he was fully prepared to find that it went against
Almagro. Pronounced guilty of levying war against the
Crown, of entering into conspiracy with the Inca, and of
dispossessing the King's governor of his city of Cuzco,
he was condemned to suffer death. Hernando called
them to witness that, before God, he had discharged his
conscience by submitting the matter to their final judgment. Though he had given it as his conviction, that

if this thing were not done the land would be lost, and the lives of all imperilled, he had expressed at the same time his belief that they, the members of the council, would pronounce an honest and unbiassed opinion. They probably understood the real significance of Hernando's disclaimer of responsibility, and replied, that meriting death as Almagro did, it was well to pass sentence upon him, and to carry out the sentence, as otherwise they would be involved in a serious calamity.

All that night, says the historian, Hernando Pizarro kept two hundred men in his quarters, to meet any attack which Pedro de Candia might be emboldened to deliver, and at early morn he repaired to Almagro, advising him that it was necessary for completing the process that he should make his confession. This he did, and admitted the justice of the accusations brought against him, while offering various excuses for, and explanations of, different parts of his conduct.

The confession completed, formal sentence was recorded against him, and a friar was employed to prepare him for death. He was greatly overcome by the announcement; old and enfeebled, he still clung to life, and vehemently protested against the injustice done him. He appealed, he said, to the Emperor; but Hernando would not permit the appeal to be received. Then he solicited an interview w th his stern adversary, and with the most piteous supplications besought him to spare his life. He reminded him of his old and long association with his brother, and the services he had rendered him and his family in their earlier career. He alluded to his labours in the cause of his king and country, and implored him to spare his grey hairs, and not to deprive him of the short remnant of an existence from which his enemies had now nothing more to fear. Hernando replied that he was surprised to see Almagro comport himself in a manner so unworthy of a brave cavalier. His fate was no worse than had befallen many a soldier before him ; and, since God had given him the grace to be a Christian, he should make use of the brief time remaining to him to close his account with heaven.* Almagro continued his entreaties, reminding Hernando of his clemency towards himself. "'Twas a hard requital," he said, "for having spared his life so recently under similar circumstances, and that, too, when he had been repeatedly urged by those around him to take it away." He concluded by asking him to consider his age and infirmities, and begging him to allow his appeal to the Emperor, so that he might spend in prison the few sad days which might still be his to repent of, and mourn over, his sins. In vain: the stern captain quitted the apartment, and gave orders that the priest should attend to receive Almagro's confession. But no confession would Almagro make unless Hernando granted him another interview. Hernando reluctantly conceded it, for he was not without compassion, though stern of purpose; and he declared that, though Almagro's crimes, had been very great, he would not have sentenced him but have sent him to the Emperor, had it not been for the constant intrigues of his partisans. He added, some-

* This speech is recorded by Herrera, but its authenticity may well be doubted. Hernando was cruel, but not brutal.

what scornfully, an expression of his wonder that a man of his proved courage should show so much fear of death. Almagro gently replied—and it is the best and most touching speech of his upon record—that since our Lord Jesus Christ feared death, it was not to be marvelled at if he, a man and a sinner, feared it. He spoke, however, to deaf ears; his doom was fixed. And when he saw that it was so, like the Duke of Monmouth, after grovelling at the feet of James II., he recovered all his fortitude and manly spirit, and calmly prepared to meet his end. He made his confession; bequeathed his estates and treasure to the Emperor; and, as the royal grant empowered him to name his successor in the governorship, he devolved the office on his son, appointing Diego de Alvarado as administrator of the province during his son's minority. Through the intercession of some of the Spanish cavaliers, and perhaps from fear of an outbreak on the part of the Almagrists, he was spared the disgrace of a public execution, and put to death in his prison by the *garotte*. His body was afterwards exhibited in the great square, when, in fulfilment of the original sentence, his head was cut off. A herald proclaimed the crimes for which he had suffered; and his remains were afterwards conveyed to the house of his friend Hernan Ponce de Leon (July 8th, 1538). On the following day they were interred in the church of Our Lady of Mercy, and, as if to show that he had been actuated by no motive of private vengeance, Hernando Pizarro, with his brother Gonzalo, attended the funeral among the principal mourners.

The execution of Almagro remains as an indelible blot on the fame of Hernando Pizarro. Not that Almagro was innocent of the crimes imputed to him. It is certain that he violated the conditions imposed by the Emperor in taking forcible possession of the city of Cuzco. To further his own ends, he was ready to enter into an alliance with the Inca which might have fatally imperilled the interests of Spain. He invaded the jurisdiction of the King's governor, and took up arms against him. It is difficult to say what more he could have done than he did to justify the charge of treason which Hernando raised. But his trial was an exercise of arbitrary authority which cannot be defended. Hernando was not even in his brother's position ; he held no warrant or official jurisdiction from the Crown ; and it was obviously his duty to have transferred his prisoner to Los Reyes, whence he might have been sent to Spain to be tried by a proper tribunal. Moreover, when he himself was in Almagro's hands, his life had been spared under circumstances of considerable provocation, and the remembrance of this fact should have made him unwilling to incur the reproach of ingratitude. Yet, when all this has been admitted, the impartial historian will find some excuse, if no justification, for Hernando's action. Almagro had given grave cause of offence. It was not only that Pizarro had conquered Peru by his own indomitable tenacity and inexhaustible courage ; it was not only that he held his governorship direct from the Crown ; it was not only that Almagro had not been unfairly treated in the division of honours and territories ; but that in the position of

O

the Spaniards in Peru such disloyalty as his might have involved the whole colony in irreparable ruin. To Hernando Pizarro, at least, this was only too evident, and we believe that in ordering the execution of Almagro he consulted no private feeling, but was honestly actuated by a regard for the public interest.

We confess ourselves unable to understand Mr. Prescott's partiality for this very small and vulgar hero, whose chief recommendation seems to have been a certain free-handedness which ensured his popularity with the common soldiers. History records no examples of the excellent qualities with which Mr. Prescott credits him. To call him "the hero of a hundred battles" is a more than poetical exaggeration; for, in truth, he had but small experience of warfare. He showed no skill as a leader of men, no capacity as a military commander, no ability as an administrator, and it is certain that by him the conquest of Peru could never have been accomplished. He did not even accomplish the conquest of Chili, and in all his expeditions committed the most serious and signal errors. The truth would seem to be that to invest the portrait of Pizarro with the desired shadows, it was necessary to illuminate that of Almagro with imaginary lights; and yet his eulogist after all is constrained to admit that it is doubtful whether he possessed "those uncommon qualities, either as a warrior or a man, that, in ordinary circumstances, would have raised him to distinction." It may safely be asserted that, had it not been linked with Pizarro's, his name would never have passed the lips of men.

CHAPTER VII.

EXPEDITION OF GONZALO PIZARRO, AND DISCOVERY OF
THE RIVER AMAZON.

N receiving intelligence of the victory of Las
Salinas, the Marquis Pizarro set out from Los
Reyes for Cuzco. At Xauxa he was met by
Almagro's son Diego, whom Hernando had
sent to the coast, and found him under
grievous alarm and anxiety as to his father's probable
fate. He received him kindly, and reassured him by
his earnest declarations that no harm should befall his
father, between whom and himself, he said, he hoped the
old friendship might be re-established. The young man
then went on his way to Los Reyes, where, by Pizarro',
orders, he was lodged in his house, and treated as his son.

It was not until he reached the Bridge of Abançay
that the Marquis heard of the execution of Almagro.
He was profoundly affected by the news, for which he
was wholly unprepared; and he stood for a long time,
with his eyes fixed on the ground, weeping. Mr. Prescotts
absolutely without foundation, holds him equally account-
able with Hernando for the death of his associate. He

chooses to suppose that he was perfectly aware of all that took place at Cuzco, and in communication with his brother respecting Almagro's fate. But this was impossible. Almagro's capture, sentence, and execution followed in such quick succession that there could have been no time for messengers to pass between the two cities. For our own part, we doubt whether, even if it had been possible, Hernando would have consulted his brother, of whose friendship for Almagro he was well aware. It is worthy of notice that whenever Hernando was on the stage, the Marquis played a more or less subordinate part. Hernando had not the wonderful tenacity, the extraordinary perseverance and patience of Francisco; but, in some respects, his was the stronger character. His will was certainly more powerful, and he always prevailed in whatever course he advocated. As to the relations between Almagro and the Marquis, some writers charge the latter with gross ingratitude; but it does not appear that the charge has any real justification. It was Pizarro who bore the burden and heat of the day, and he was certainly entitled to the larger reward. When all America was supposed to be teeming with gold and silver, he no doubt thought that Almagro's southern territory would yield him a treasure equal to that which Peru had yielded; and the Court of Spain appears to have considered the division equitable. The tendency of most historians is either to whitewash an historical personage until no speck or stain can be detected on his armour, or to blacken him until he stands repulsive in a mask of inordinate hideousness.

Pizarro has been chosen to undergo the latter process, but really without affording sufficient grounds. He was not an angel of light, but he was not a monster of darkness. He was a man of many merits and some failings; like most of his race and time, he placed no great value upon human life, nor was he over scrupulous in the fulfilment of promises. But, on the whole, he did not treat Almagro unfairly; he showed himself, on more than one occasion, mindful of their long association and old comradeship; and we believe that Almagro's life would have been spared if he had reached Cuzco earlier. As a mere matter of policy, he would have seen that the death of Almagro did not mean the annihilation of Almagro's faction, and that it could not fail to be resented by the Court of Spain as an illegal exercise of authority.

The Marquis considered it advisable, in support of his office, to make a public entry into Cuzco, at the head of his train of cavaliers, with the pomp of banners and amid the martial music of trumpets and clarions. He found both his brothers absent on an expedition against the Indians in the vicinity of Lake Titicaca. On their return, he despatched Gonzalo to undertake the subjugation of the tribes of Charcas; and when he had accomplished the difficult task, rewarded him and Hernando with a grant of land in the neighbourhood of Porco, known to be rich in minerals. Hernando worked the mines with much skill and on an extensive scale, but did not discover the vast treasures of silver Potosi which, all unknown to him, lay, with their "potentiality of wealth," within his limits. As soon as he had amassed

a sufficient fortune, he prepared to return to Spain and
defend himself against the charges which, at Court,
Diego de Alvarado and other partisans of the unfortunate
Almagro were pressing against him. Before his departure he strongly advised his brother to beware of the
"men of Chili," as the Almagrists were called ; desperate
men, he said, who would allow nothing to interfere
between them and their revenge. He urged him not to
allow them to assemble in any number within fifty miles
of his person, and to maintain always and everywhere a
strong bodyguard. " I shall not be here," he added,
with a touch of pathos, "to watch over you." But
Pizarro, who was far from being suspicious, made light
of his brother's alarms. There was no cause, he said,
for fear ; moreover, every hair on the head of Almagro's
followers was a guarantee for his safety.

Hernando Pizarro embarked at Los Reyes in the
summer of 1539. He reached the Spanish coast in
safety, and proceeded to Valladolid, where he met with
but a cold reception. Diego de Alvarado had been
before him, and he who first tells his tale has always an
advantage over the later comer. Hernando, however,
was nothing disheartened, and by dint of repetition of
his justification, and by, we may assume, a judicious
distribution of presents, he suspended for awhile the
opinion of his judges. The delay so irritated Diego
de Alvarado that he endeavoured to settle the points
at issue by challenging Hernando to mortal combat.
The challenge fell to the ground through the sudden
death of the challenger which happened within five days

Pizarro, however, did not wholly escape. On the ground that by releasing the Inca Manco he had facilitated the Indian rebellion, and because he had violated the law by his execution of Almagro, he was deprived of his order of Santiago, and thrown into prison at Medina del Campo, where he was detained for twenty years. In 1560 he obtained his release, and was allowed to spend the remainder of his long life in the tranquil enjoyment of a considerable fortune. He lived to the ripe old age of one hundred years.

The Marquis was now the sole ruler of Peru; but he had much difficult and laborious work to accomplish before his authority could be considered as firmly established. Encouraged by the feuds which had broken out among his conquerors, the Inca Manco quitted his mountain fastnesses, and with a considerable force posted himself in the sierra between Cuzco and the coast; maintaining a warfare resembling that of the Scotch borderers in the troublous old times of the long struggle between England and Scotland; making sudden forays on the plantations of the Spanish settlers, burning their houses and granaries, carrying off their cattle, and murdering men, women, and children who fell into his hands. Several detachments were sent against him, but these he defeated, or ensnaring them in an ambush, cut them to pieces. Pizarro, therefore, placed a considerable force under his brother Gonzalo, and ordered him to march against this persevering foe. Whenever the Spaniards brought him to bay, they defeated him, but his knowledge of the country always enabled him to effect his escape; and the Marquis found himself compelled to adopt a different policy. For this purpose he established settlements in the heart of the disaffected country—settlements which assumed the character of military colonies. "The houses were usually built of stone, to which were added the various public offices, and sometimes a fortress. A municipal corporation was organized. Settlers were invited by the distribution of large tracts of land in the neighbourhood, with a stipulated number of Indian vassals to each. The soldiers then gathered there, sometimes accompanied by their wives and families; for the women of Castile seem to have disdained the impediments of sex, in the ardour of conjugal attachment, or, it may be, of romantic adventure. A populous settlement rapidly grew up in the wilderness, affording protection to the surrounding territory, and furnishing a commercial *depôt* for the country, and an armed force ready at all times to maintain public order."

Among the settlements thus formed were the Villa de la Plata, or "City of Silver," in the mining district of Charcas; Guamanga, midway between Lima and Cuzco; and Arequipa, on the shore of the Southern Sea.

The force of character and rough mental activity of Pizarro were strikingly illustrated by his labours at this period—labours which would have been remarkable in any man, but were specially remarkable in a man who had received no liberal culture, and from his youth up had been engaged in arduous and difficult enterprises. Returning from Cuzco to Los Reyes, he addressed himself to the task of encouraging the development of the resources of the country. To agricultural industry he paid special attention, and had the sagacity to import the seeds of the different European grains, which, before long, yielded luxuriant crops. He took measures to facilitate commercial intercourse with the Spanish colonies lying north of Peru. He sedulously promoted the working of the mines, which already began to make such returns that the commonest articles of life fetched extravagant prices, and the only things of small value seemed to be the precious metals themselves. But as these changed hands they found their way to Spain, and rose to their true standard as they passed into the general European currency. So the Spaniards discovered that after years of adventure and suffering they had found at last that Land of Gold and Silver, that long-dreamed-of " El Dorado," which had inspired men to such deeds of noble note. In rapidly increasing numbers emigrants entered the country, and extending in every direction, gradually assured the supremacy of the Spanish government.

This influx of adventurers enabled Pizarro to carry out his projects for the fuller colonization of the country. He despatched Pedro de Valdivia on an expedition to conquer Chili, which proved entirely successful; and his brother Gonzalo to the southern district of Callao, after which he sent him to discover the region of cinnamon that was supposed to lie beyond the Andes.

Gonzalo Pizarro has been described as, in ability and breadth of view, inferior to his two elder brothers.

Neither did he show himself equally "cool and crafty" in his policy; but he was equally resolute, intrepid, and energetic. He had a handsome person, open and engaging features, a free soldier-like address, and a generous temper; so that he was the idol of his followers. His spirit was high and adventurous, and he had the faculty, so important in a leader of men, of being able to infuse that spirit into others, and thus almost to ensure the success of any enterprise he undertook. He was an excellent captain, prompt in decision, fertile in resources, and calm and self-reliant in the hour of danger. His expedition across the Andes calls for a brief notice in these pages.

In order to increase his brother's authority, Pizarro appointed him Governor of Quito, and in January 1540 he set out from the capital of his government with three hundred and fifty Spaniards and four thousand Indian auxiliaries. Of the Spanish division one hundred and fifty were mounted. All were well equipped; the supplies were abundant; and to guard against famine, an immense herd of swine followed in the rear of the army. At first the route presented no obstacles; but on entering the province of Quixos, Gonzalo plunged into the ravines of the Andes, and difficulties beset him at every step. As he ascended into the loftier regions, his army suffered much from the icy winds that swept down the rugged declivities of the mountain-range; and great alarm was caused by a sudden and tremendous earthquake, which seemed to threaten the disruption of the entire mountain-system. In one place the earth was rent asunder by

Nature's violent agony, while streams of sulphurous water poured forth, and a large village was toppled headlong into the abyss.

They experienced a change of climate as they descended the eastern slopes of the Cordilleras, and, in the lowlands, were almost suffocated by the intense heat ; while day after day, and night after night, storms of thunder a id lightning, issuing from the gorges of the sierra, beat about their laborious path. For upwards of six weeks they made their way through a deluge of rain, until, wet to the skin and weary with incessant toil, they could scarcely drag along their feeble limbs. After wading through many a swamp and mountain-torrent, they reached a country which they called *Canelas*, "Land of Cinnamon." It was covered with immense forests of trees bearing the fragrant and precious bark, but their remoteness from the ordinary channels of commerce rendered them valueless to the discoverers. From the natives, however, they learned that at a distance of ten days' journey lay a fair and fertile region, abounding in gold, and inhabited by populous natives. Thither, though he had already reached the limits fixed by the Marquis for his expedition, Gonzalo Pizarro resolved to lead his soldiers, who, on their part, wherever he led were well content to follow.

Pursuing their adventurous march, they entered upon broad tracts of gum savannahs, terminated by forests, which, as they drew near, seemed to assume the likeness of an impenetrable barrier of vegetation. Trees of stupendous height and girth, some of them measuring thirty feet, and more, in diameter, were hung with festoons of

tiarras and creepers, which spread from bough to bough,
and interwound with one another, and rose high above
even the highest trunk, to blend in one vast green canopy,
while beneath flourished a mighty jungle of ferns and
bushes and undergrowth of every kind, through which
the traveller was forced to hew his way with axe or
sword. The passage of this luxuriant tropical wilderness
was a grievous trial to Pizarro's little army. Their provisions, spoiled by the weather, had long since failed, and
the live-stock they had taken with them had perished or
been consumed, or had made their escape in the woods
and mountain-passes. They had with them at their departure from Quito nearly a thousand dogs, including
some of that fine breed of bloodhounds which in the West
Indian Islands had been used for hunting down the natives.
On these they lived for awhile, though their lean carcasses
furnished but a sorry food ; afterwards they subsisted as
best they could on the herbs, berries, and roots which
they gathered in the forests.

At last Pizarro reached a town and country called Coca,
which was inhabited by a more civilized and kindly race,
so that he was able to recruit his men with liberal supplies
of provisions. After resting for nearly two months he
resumed his march, and reached the banks of the broad
Napo, one of the main branches of the great Amazonian
system of rivers. Along its verdurous banks he took his
way, in the hope that they would afford a practicable route,
but found the density of the thickets, which descended
to the very edge of the water, a serious impediment. After
proceeding for about fifty leagues, the Spaniards suddenly

heard an awful rushing noise, such as they had never heard before. For six leagues further they advanced, while the din constantly increased, and the furious river surged past them in flashing rapids, growing ever more and more violent, until they came to a point where it suddenly hurled its flood of waters over a precipice twelve hundred feet in height,* and filled the air with masses of glittering foam. " The appalling sounds," says Prescott,† "which they had heard for the distance of six leagues, were rendered yet more oppressive to the spirits by the gloomy stillness of the surrounding forests. The rude warriors were filled with sentiments of awe. . . . No living thing was to be seen but the wild te·ants of the wilderness—the unwieldy boa, and the loathsome alligator basking on the borders of the stream. The trees towering in wide-spread magnificence towards the heavens, the river rolling on in its rocky bed as it had rolled for ages, the solitude and silence of the scene, broken only by the hoarse fall of waters or the faint rustling of the woods,— all seemed to spread out around them in the same wild and primitive state as when they came from the hands of the Creator."

At a distance of forty leagues from this wonderful " fall of waters," the Spaniards saw with surprise that the great river so contracted its volume as to pass through a narrow cutting in the rock, not more than twenty feet broad. At this point they resolved to effect their passage to the other

* This estimate is the exaggeration suggested by the excited imagination of the travellers.

† Prescott's "Conquest of Peru," ii., 144, 145.

side, and constructed a sufficient bridge by throwing the huge trunks of trees across the chasm, which, narrow as it was, descended to the dizzy depth of two hundred fathoms. The men and horses crossed in safety ; only one life was lost, that of a soldier, who, venturing to look down into the awful gloom, turned giddy, lost his footing, and was seen no more.

After putting to flight a band of hostile Indians, the Spaniards entered a region called Guema, wretched in its poverty, utterly without resources, and scantily peopled, where they were again compelled to sustain nature on the meagre fare of herbs, roots, and the young buds of trees. Death and disease were busy among them, but Pizarro held on his dauntless way, deceived by the *ignis fatuus* of a rich and fertile country, which constantly moved before his imagination. He came at last into a country which was less savagely inhospitable than the barren Guema; a country where the Indians lived in huts, clothed themselves in cotton garments, and cultivated crops of maize. To his wayworn and half-famished soldiers, who had lost everything but their courage, it seemed a veritable Eden,—that earthly Paradise of which most of us, in our lifetime, enjoy at least a brief experience ; and they were well please l to linger among its groves and fields as long as seemed good to their restless commander. To him, after surveying the country round about, and finding it to be a region of swamp and lake, of stream and forest, came the thought of constructing a brigantine, on board of which he might embark his invalids and baggage. It was a bold thought, and to carry it into execution was a bold task. To obtain the needful ironwork it was necessary to erect a forge ; and as it was the rainy season, all the work had to be done under cover. For fuel he cut down the trees of the forest ; nails he obtained from the shoes of the horses which had died on the march, or been killed for food. Instead of pitch he used gum distilled from the trees ; for oakum he made use of the rags and tatters of the uniforms of his soldiers. Robinson Crusoe himself displayed not more ingenuity in his imaginary island than Gonzalo Pizarro on the banks of the Napo. He not only projected, but he executed ; he laboured with his hands as zealously as any one of his men ; now at the forge, now in the wood, now making charcoal, now collecting resin. His example inspired his men to surpass them-selves in willing industry and cheerful endurance ; and in less than two months the brigantine was completed, and launched upon the broad waters of the Napo.

The command was given to a cavalier of Trujillo, one Francisco de Orellana, of whose courage and capacity Gonzalo had a high opinion, and on whose loyalty to himself he placed full reliance. The sick were embarked, and the baggage, and the expedition was then resumed ; Gonzalo Pizarro bravely marching at the head of his soldiers along the river bank ; while the brigantine, and four canoes which had also been constructed, slowly sailed down the stream. Frequently the army crossed from one side to the other, by means of this flotilla, when the passage through the forest became very difficult, and the transit generally occupied a couple of days. In this way they progressed slowly and wearily for week after week, always looking forward to that land of golden abundance which they never reached. The further they advanced, the further they seemed to recede. Hunger again cast its gaunt shadow over their path. All their provisions had long ago been consumed; they had devoured the last of their horses; they were reduced to gnaw at the leather of their belts and saddles—to feed upon toads, serpents, lizards—to stifle the pangs of appetite with roots and herbs and berries.*

For two months Gonzalo and his followers persevered in their painful enterprise. Then they learned of a rich and populous country, at ten days' journey, where the river they had followed so long (the Napo) poured its waters into a greater river, which flowed towards the east. This intelligence they gathered partly by signs and partly by some words and phrases which Pizarro's Indians were able to interpret. After some consideration, Gonzalo re-solved to halt his weary men, who were spent with fatigue and hunger, and send Orellana, with the brigantine, down to the meeting of the waters, to obtain supplies, and, after landing the sick and the baggage, to return with them to Gonzalo and the army. Orellana, with fifty soldiers, pushed off into mid-stream, where the current was swiftest, and sailed away with such rapidity that in three days he accomplished eighty leagues. He reached the point of confluence, but instead of a fertile and hospitable country,

---

"Yeruas y rayzes, y fruta siluestre, sapos, y culebras, y otras malas sauandijas, si las auia por aquellas montañas que todo les hazia buen estomago a los Españoles ; que peor les yua con la falta de cosas tan viles."—*Garcilasso la Vega*, "Com. Real ," pt. 2, lib. iii., c. 4.

found one that was barren and desolate. There were no
provisions accessible, he could scarcely find sustenance for
himself. What then was to be done? To force his way up
the river, against a current of such extraordinary violence,
would occupy a twelvemonth; should he abandon his
barque and return by land to his leader's camp? The
latter was the only alternative possible to an honourable
cavalier with a sense of duty; but unfortunately, in all the
Spanish expeditions, a demoralising influence got abroad,
weakening the ties between men and officers, between
officers and commander. Every adventurer was always
seeking to gain the mastery for himself. So it came to
pass that Orellana conceived the idea of throwing off
Pizarro's authority; and he proposed to his followers that
they should abandon their countrymen in the forest, sail
down the mighty river formed by the junction of the Napo
and the Coca,—a river running through lands of immense
wealth,—and, gaining the great ocean, return to Spain,
laden with glory and treasure. At first, this gross and
cowardly desertion of their chief and their comrades-
in-arms was scouted by Orellana's company, but by
degrees the prospect of new adventures and great gain,
and the certainty of deliverance from their present wretchedness, converted to his views all but a single cavalier,
Hernan Sanchez de Vargas. "Among the faithless, faithful only he!" Procuring his election as captain, Orellana
began his daring voyage, leaving Vargas alone in the
great wilderness—to die, it might be, a martyr to duty.
The brigantine sailed rapidly, and, favoured by fortune,
escaped all the perils which beset the navigation of the

P

Amazon. Many times she was in danger of being wrecked on its rocks or in its rapids, but she threaded her way securely. The bold mariners were frequently harassed by the warlike tribes on the borders of the river, who attacked them whenever they attempted to land, and followed in their wake in their canoes. Some of them were accompanied in fight by their women, who bent their bows with vigour ; hence, with a remembrance of the old Greek legend, the Spaniards called that country the land of the Amazons.

Orellana and his men were the first of the human race to cross the vast Southern Continent from east to west, and descend the mighty river Amazon, a voyage of two thousand five hundred miles. Reaching the ocean, Orellana sailed to the Island of Cubaqua or Trinidad, where, with the riches put on board the brigantine, he purchased a vessel, and sailed to Spain. At court he was well received ; his gifts procured him a friendly hearing, and his narrative of the wonderful discoveries he had made a royal licence to fit out a new expedition. The great river which he had successfully navigated received his name, and was long known as the Orellana, though now men call it, less appropriately, the Amazon. The spirit of adventure still glowed in the breasts of the Spaniards, and he quickly found himself at the head of five hundred men, eager to carve out their fortunes in the heart of South America. But his treachery met at last with its Nemesis ; he died on the outward passage, and the lands which he had discovered eventually fell into the hands of Portugal. If we cannot admit, with Robertson that the base crime he committed "is, in some measure, balanced by the glory of having ventured upon a navigation of near two thousand leagues, through unknown nations, in a vessel hastily constructed with green timber, and by very unskilful hands, without provisions, without a compass or a pilot,"—if we cannot admit that success can ever wash out the stain of an evil deed, we may nevertheless do justice to the stern and self-reliant courage which dictated such an enterprise, and the patient intrepidity which conducted it to a fortunate termination.*

Let us return to Gonzalo Pizarro. Weeks elapsed, and there was no sign of Orellana or the brigantine. Reconnoitring parties were despatched in search of them, but returned without any intelligence. It does not seem to have occurred to Pizarro that his lieutenant had

---

* " His courage and alacrity supplied every defect. Committing himself fearlessly to the guidance of the stream, the Napo bore him along to the south, until he reached the great channel of the Maragnon. Turning with it towards the coast, he held on his course in that direction. He made frequent descents on both sides of the river, sometimes seizing by force of arms the provisions of the fierce savages seated on its banks, and sometimes procuring a supp'y of food by a friendly intercourse with more gentle tribes. After a long series of dangers, which he encountered with amazing fortitude, and of distresses which he supported with no less magnanimity, he reached the ocean, where new perils awaited him. These he likewise surmounted, and got safe to the Spanish settlement in the island of Cubagua ; from thence he sailed to Spain. The vanity natural to travellers who visit regions unknown to the rest of mankind, and the art of an adventurer solicitous to magnify his own merit, concurred in prompting him to mingle an extraordinary proportion of the marvellous in the narrative of his voyage. He pretended to have discovered nations so rich that the roofs of their temples were covered

deserted him; but, after a long delay, he came to the conclusion that Orellana had been unable to ascend the river, in consequence of the strength and velocity of its current, and he resolved therefore to make his way to the junction of the rivers, in the hope he should find him established there with an abundance of provisions. By his example and his cheerful speeches he encouraged his men to construct some canoes and rafts; and then, partly by land and partly by water, he conveyed them over the distance of two hundred leagues to the spot where the Napo pours its tributary waters into the mightiest of American rivers. The journey occupied two months, and involved a pitiful sacrifice of life; and what was the dismay, the anger of the survivors, when they fell in with their half-starved comrade, Sanchez de Vargas, and learned from him the story of Orellana's

with plates of gold, and described a republic of women so warlike and powerful, as to have extended their dominion over a considerable tract of the fertile plains which he had visited. Extravagant as those gains were, they gave rise to an opinion that a region abounding with gold, distinguished by the name of *El Dorado*, and a community of Amazons, were to be found in this part of the New World; and such is the propensity of mankind to believe what is wonderful, that it has been slowly and with difficulty that reason and observation have exploded those fables. The voyage, however, even when stripped of every romantic embellishment, deserves to be recorded not only as one of the most memorable occurrences in that adventurous age, but as the first event which led to any certain knowledge of the extensive countries that stretch eastward from the Andes to the ocean."—*Robertson,* "Conquest of America," iii.. 349. 350. The "Expedition of Gonzalo Pizarro" and the "Voyage de Francesco de Orellana" have been edited for the Hakluyt Society (1859) by Mr. Clement R. Markham, with valuable notes.

treachery! The stoutest veteran felt his heart sink within him : only Gonzalo Pizarro maintained his usual courage and resolution, and with heroic spirit faced the terrible difficulties that surrounded them. He sought to reassure his followers by praising them for the constancy and patience they had exhibited; he sought to inspire them by dwelling on the old traditions of Castile. They were twelve hundred leagues from Quito, it was true ; well, what was their obvious course? To return to Quito : what they had already done they could do again. To remain in the heart of the wilderness, or to advance further eastward, was equally impossible ; this, then, was their sole resource, and he bade them adopt it without hesitation. He spoke of the immortal renown with which such an achievement would invest their names. He would lead them back, he said, by another route, and it might well be assumed that sooner or later they would come upon that land of teeming plenty of which they had so often heard ; and they would have, at least, this reflection to console them, that every league they accomplished would be a league nearer home. Let them act but as men and soldiers; let them put aside unmanly fears and despondency; the brave heart would support and strengthen the failing body ; difficulties met in the right spirit were already half conquered !

To this ardent speech, the speech of a man of the true heroic temper,* Pizarro's soldiers listened with eagerness. It is natural for all of us to breathe more freely when we

* It is noticeable that all the Pizarros were men of mark ; Gonzalo and Hernando must have risen anywhere into fame and influence.

find our leader confident and self-reliant. A battle is seldom lost if the commander is seen to feel assured of victory. Moreover the force of Pizarro's conclusion could not be doubted. It was evident that the course he advised was the only course that promised even a chance of safety; and the soldiers, as they prepared to adopt it, felt kindling within them a glow of Castilian pride. They, the sons of the warriors who had humbled the Crescent on many a battlefield, would show themselves worthy of their ancestors in fortitude and courage. The enthusiasm of their leader communicated itself—for enthusiasm is contagious—to their own bosoms, especially as they put their entire trust in him, and knew and owned that he deserved their devotion; for from the very beginning of the expedition he had been foremost in its perils and its labours. He had shared with them in their privations, and instead of claiming the privileges of his rank, had thrown in his lot with the meanest soldier. He had borne his part in the toil and burden of the march; he had given of his own miserable allowance to his famished followers; he had gently and patiently ministered to the wants of the sick; and with all this, he had shown not only the qualities of a generous comrade, but those of an able captain; he had repressed disorder, encouraged the despondent, and rewarded the brave; he had been cool and calm in danger, undaunted by difficulty, fertile in resource.

Striking somewhat to the north, Gonzalo Pizarro led his little band of followers through a country less beset with difficulties than that which they had previously traversed. But it must be remembered that such distresess as they encountered, their increasing feebleness rendered them less and less able to endure. Their only sustenance was the scanty food they collected in the forest, or were able to obtain in the scattered Indian settlements. Piiful was the fate of those whose strength gave way, for nothing could be done to help them, and with a sad heart Pizarro was forced to leave them to perish in the wilderness. The survivors persevered, though their failing limbs could scarcely drag along their attenuated bodies, and they seemed rather a company of spectres, let loose from some region of awe and terror, than the remains of a gallant body of Spanish cavaliers and fighting men. They persevered; and in June 1542, after an absence of more than two years, once again assembled on the lofty plains in the neighbourhood of Quito. But how different, as it has been said,—how different their aspect from that which they had worn when issuing from the gates of the same capital to commence their expedition, with high romantic hope and in all the bravery of military array! Their horses gone; their weapons broken, rusted, or thrown aside because they were too weak to carry them; their shrunken limbs imperfectly clothed with the skins of wild beasts; their long, matted, and uncleansed locks hanging wildly down upon their shoulders; many of them grey and grizzled with anxiety and suffering and want; their faces burned and darkened by exposure to the tropical sun; their bodies wasted and weakened by famine, and sorely disfigured with scars—one might have supposed that the charnel-house had disgorged its inmates, as they plodded forward drearily, with the wandering, uncertain step of men drunken or dizzy! Of the four thousand Indians who had accompanied Pizarro from Quito more than half had perished; of the Spaniards only eighty returned.

The Christian settlers in Quito, hearing of their arrival, came out to meet them, and with a curious exhibition of sympathy, on perceiving their destitute appearance, partially stripped themselves of their own clothes, that their countrymen might not be too painfully reminded of the depth of wretchedness to which they had sunk. They listened, with tears, to the pathetic tale they had to tell, and re-entered the town in company with them; all hasting, as if moved by one common impulse, to the church, where they offered their devout thanksgivings to the Almighty Providence that had miraculously preserved them through so long a succession of perils.

Thus ended the expedition to the Amazon, in which, it must be owned, Gonzalo Pizarro proved himself worthy of the eulogium passed upon him by an historian by no means partial to his family: "Finalmente, Gonçalo Piçarro entró en el Quito, triunfando del valor, i sufrimiento, i de la constancia, recto, é immutable vigor del animo, pues hombres humanos no se hallan haver tanto safrido, ni padecido tantas desventuras."*

* Herrera, "Historia General," dec. vii., lib. iii., c. 14. Herrera is by no means a safe authority as regards the career and conduct of the Pizarros. He seems to have derived his facts from informants strongly prejudiced against them. Many of his statements are apparently the offspring of a vivid imagination, and the speeches which he puts into the mouths of his personages are often inconsistent with their true character.

If the tale the followers of Pizarro had to tell to the people of Quito was a strange and stirring one, they, in return, had a story to relate which could not fail to astonish its hearers. When Gonzalo left Quito in 1540, his brother the Marquis was sole ruler of Peru, wielding an apparently unquestioned authority, which, with characteristic vigour and energy, he was extending into newly conquered territories. He returned, in 1542, to find the government in the hands of a stranger, Blasco Nuñez Vela, who as viceroy held his commission from the King; and to learn that his brother, the conqueror of Peru, had perished by the assassin's dagger in a quarrel with the Almagrist faction.

The chain of events that led to this tragical occurrence we shall now proceed to trace.

CHAPTER VIII.

USIED in the development of the resources of the country, and in fostering and protecting the interests of the Spanish colonists, the Marquis gave but little heed to the proceedings of the Almagrist faction. Whether it was that he despised them, or considered it hopeless to attempt their conciliation, or was over-confident in his ability to foil their machinations, certain it is that he treated them with profound indifference. Or it may be that, conscious of his innocence of the death of Almagro, he did not suppose that their vengeance would be directed against one who had given them no special cause of complaint. At all events, he made no attempt either to attach them to his side, or to crush them utterly. He allowed them to go where they would and do as they would, so that before long upwards of two hundred of these "men of Chili" (as they were called) gathered in Los Reyes, where they found a suitable leader in Almagro's former major domo, Juan de Rada ; and a centre of hope, pride, and ambition in the young Almagro, who was now grown up to the age of manhood, and was gifted with all the qualities

that secure the affections of soldiers. He was bold,
liberal, frank of speech and manner, of a graceful person,
and skilled in all martial exercises. That the Marquis
should have permitted so dangerous a rival to remain in
Los Reyes, and to have drawn around him a group of
needy and desperate cavaliers, is a proof that he was
by no means so astute and suspicious as some English
historians have represented. He has been censured for
not purchasing their support for himself by presents and
favours, but it seems to be forgotten that he could have
done so only at the expense of his own loyal adherents.
There is no evidence that they were in any way debarred
from earning a decorous livelihood like any other
Spaniards, and the truth seems to be that they had so
long lived upon Almagro's lavish and thoughtless bounty,
that any kind of industry had become irksome to them.
Their extreme poverty is frequently illustrated by a
repetition of Herrera's absurd anecdote, that twelve
cavaliers, formerly officers of distinction under Almagro,
lodged in the same house, and having but one cloak
amongst them, wore it alternately ; he whose turn it was
to appear in public donning it for the occasion, while the
rest, for want of a decent dress, remained at home. The
anecdote is obviously a fiction. We can find no evidence
that the Marquis confiscated the property of any of the
men of Chili ; and it is certain that even the young
Almagro was suffered to retain a considerable portion of
his father's estates.

The greater the indulgence with which Pizarro treated
them, the bolder waxed the men of Chili. They felt no

gratitude to the Governor for sparing their lives—for not restraining their freedom, but were continually plotting the means of overthrowing him, and elevating the young Almagro in his place. The friends of Pizarro warmly remonstrated with him for his excess of leniency, and warned him to be on his guard against the enemies who were secretly aiming at his destruction. " Poor devils ! " he replied, " fortune has behaved to them but scurvily, we will not trouble them further." And he went about freely, despising even the commonest precautions ; without an attendant he would ride to all parts of the town, and even into the neighbouring country.

While the Almagrists were thus engaged in weaving the meshes of secret conspiracy, tidings reached Los Reyes that the Court of Spain had appointed Vaca de Castro as a special judge or commissioner to inquire into the affairs of Peru. The Marquis was disturbed by the unexpected intelligence ; but he gave orders that the representative of the Crown should receive a splendid welcome when he landed, and that fitting accommodation should be prepared for him on his route. Great was the exultation of the Almagrists, for they confidently antici-pated that the new functionary would revenge them upon Pizarro, and they despatched one of their number, Don Alonzo de Montemayor, to meet him, and lay before him a statement of their grievances (April 1541), that he might be prepared to redress them without delay.

Months passed, however, and nothing was heard of his arrival. At last a vessel coming into port brought the intelligence that most of the ships of the royal squadron

had foundered in the heavy storms on the coast, and it
was at once assumed that Vaca de Castro had perished
with them.   This was a new disappointment to the men
of Chili, whose exasperation against Pizarro seems to
have been whetted by a calamity in which he had
obviously no share.   Their rage attained to such proportions that they no longer made an effort to conceal it.
If they met the Governor in the street they would turn
sullenly away, and neglect the ordinary courtesy of
doffing their bonnets.   On one occasion, the inhabitants
of Los Reyes found that the public pillory in the great
square had been decorated with three ropes, to which
were attached labels bearing the names of Pizarro, Velasquez, the Alcalde Mayor, and Juan Picado, the Marquis's
secretary, while the ends were so arranged as to point to
their respective houses.   We are told that Picado was
specially obnoxious to the discontented cavaliers, because
all communications to the Governor passed through his
hands, and as the latter could not read or write, it was
suspected that the secretary coloured them according to
his private likings or animosities.   However this may be,
he seems to have been of a bold and aggressive disposition ; and to show his contempt for the insult levelled
at him and his master, he rode, splendidly dressed,
through the street in which the young Almagro lived,
wearing a cap that bore in the front of it a medal of
gold embossed with a fig in silver, and the significant
label, " For the men of Chili."*   It is strange that so

* That is, a fig for the men of Chili !   See Garcilasso de la Vega,
part 2, lib. iii., c. 6.

poor a jest should have deeply incensed the Almagrist cavaliers.

The hostile feelings evinced by the faction, and their increasing desperation, attracted the attention of the Indians, and many of them conveyed secret warnings to the Marquis and his friends. It was on account of these, perhaps, the rumour arose that Pizarro had begun to purchase lances with which to re-equip his soldiers. At the same time it was observed that Juan de Rada, poor as he professed to be, had bought a new coat of mail; which, among the Spaniards, appears to have been always the precursor of some deed of violence.

With that candour which was characteristic of Pizarro, though he has been so often stigmatized as " cunning " and " crafty," he sent for Juan de Rada. We are told that when the Almagrist chief obeyed the summons he found the Marquis in his garden, inspecting some orange trees which he had caused to be planted. They reminded him probably of the fair orange-groves of his native land. " What is this, Juan de Rada," exclaimed the Marquis, " which I hear of your buying arms to kill me ? "

" Not so," answered the cavalier ; " but I have purchased two cuirasses and a coat of mail for self-defence."

" But why should you need such armour now more than at any other time ? "

" Because," replied Juan de Rada, " they tell us, and it is indeed well known, that your lordship is purchasing lances with which to slay us all. Let your lordship make an end of us ; and, indeed, as you have commenced by

destroying the head, I know not why you should have
any respect for the feet."

" It was neither thought nor deed of mine by which
Almagro fell."

" It is also said," continued Juan de Rada, "that your
lordship intends to kill the judge who is coming from
Spain ; but if such be your design, and you are resolved
to slay all the party of Almagro, at least spare Don Diego,
for I assure you he is innocent.   Banish him, and I will
accompany him wherever fortune may carry us."

At these atrocious charges the Marquis was hotly
indignant.

" Who has made you," he exclaimed, " believe of me
such vile treachery and shameful wickedness ?   Of no
such thing have I ever had any thought, and I am more
desirous than you are that this judge should come.   Nay,
he might have been here already, if he had embarked in
the galleon I sent for him.   As to the tale about the
spears, this is the truth.   The other day, when I was out
hunting, among the whole company was not to be found
one with a spear.   Therefore I ordered my servants to
buy one, and they have bought four.   Would to God !,
Juan de Rada, that the judge was here, so that these
falsehoods might have an end, and that God might make
the truth manifest."

For the time, at least, the Governor's frank address,
and open, unhesitating speech, had their influence upon
Juan de Rada.   He answered, " By heaven, my lord.
but these stories have plunged me into debt for upwards
of five hundred pesos, which I have spent in buying

Q

armour. Well, I have now, at all events, a coat of mail to defend me against any who may wish to do me harm."

" Please God, Juan de Rada," answered Pizarro, mildly, " nothing of the kind will be done by me."

Here the conversation ended, and Juan de Rada was about to take his leave, when Pizarro's jester, who had been present, remarked, " Why do you not give him some of these oranges? " For as they were the first that had been ripened by the sun of Peru, they were highly valued.

" You say well," answered the Marquis, good humouredly ; and he gathered half-a-dozen of the golden fruit and gave them to Juan de Rada, with the remark, that when he wanted anything he should come and tell him. Then Juan de Rada kissed the Marquis's hands, and the two parted apparently on the friendliest terms.

So Pizarro thought ; but the impression made on Juan de Rada by his frankness and good temper soon passed away, and he once more plunged into the projected conspiracy. Again Pizarro was apprised of the murderous designs of his enemies; he trusted, however, in the good understanding established with Juan de Rada, and the influence and authority of his position. Among others, he was cautioned by a priest, but he told him the report was without foundation ; that it was no better than an Indian saying ("decho de Indios "), and that his informant had invented it to get a horse or some other present. The same, or another priest, betook himself to Picado, and informed him that he had his information from one of the conspirators, who, in his confession, had revealed the sin that troubled him. Picado communi-

cated it to Pizarro, but the latter, as if misguided by Fate
to his own destruction, treated it as of no account. "It
is the priest's device," he said; "he wants to be made a
bishop."* After reflecting upon it, however, he deemed
it advisable to mention it to Velasquez, the Alcalde
Mayor; who, instead of ordering the arrest of the conspirators, and adopting measures to ascertain the accuracy
of the report, dismissed it lightly, with the infatuated
vaunt, "Be under no apprehension, my Lord Marquis,
of any injury befalling you so long as I hold the rod of
justice."

That same evening, as Pizarro was retiring to bed, he
was informed by his page that the general voice of the
city said he would be attacked on the following day by
the men of Chili. "Boy," he said, "these things are
not for you to talk about."

Next morning the warning was conveyed by several
pages; and Pizarro roused himself from his security so
far as to give directions to the Alcalde Mayor to arrest
the principal Almagrists. But he showed no urgency
or insistency in the notice; and as the Alcalde was
wrapped up in the false infatuation of measureless
egotism, he made no haste to act upon his instructions.

The next day was Sunday, and Pizarro's friends pre-

* "Pues un dia antes un sacerdote clerigo llamado Benao fue de
noche y avisso á Picado el secreptaro, y dixole, ' Mañana Domingo,
quando el Marquez saliere á misa, tienen concertado los de Chile de
matar al Marquez y á vos y á sus amigos. Esto me á dicho vno en
confision, para que os venga á avisar.' Pues savido esto Picado se
fue luego y lo conto al Marquez, y el le rrespondio, ' Ese clerigo
obispado quiere.'"—*Pedro Pizarro.*

vailed upon him not to go to mass, lest some sudden attack should be hazarded. After mass, the leading inhabitants of Los Reyes waited upon him to pay their respects. The *levée* occupied some time; and at its conclusion the Marquis retired to his chamber, in company with his brother Martin, his Alcalde Mayor, and his old friend, Francisco de Chaves.

Juan de Rada and his associates, early on Sunday morning, assembled in Almagro's house, and anxiously awaited the hour when the Governor should issue from the church. Their alarm and their disappointment were equally great when they heard that he had not gone to mass, as was his custom, but had remained at home, through illness, as some reported. They immediately concluded—for guilt is quick of suspicion—that their design had been detected, and that their ruin was inevitable. Contradictory opinions prevailed; some urged that they should immediately disband, in the hope that Pizarro would overlook, or might still be ignorant of, their intrigue; others proposed that they should strike the fatal blow at once. The more desperate, as is usual in such cases, carried along with them their weaker comrades. Springing from his bed, Juan de Rada hastily put on his armour, and in a few animated words called upon them to avenge the death of Almagro, and seize the supreme power in Peru, or at least to act in self-defence. With loud acclamations they responded to his appeal.*

* A somewhat different version is given by Herrera, who says that one of the band of conspirators threw open the doors, rushed out, and called on his comrades " to follow him, or he would openly

A white flag was hung from the window, as a signal to their confederates to arm and hasten to their support.*

Mr. Prescott remarks that these arrangements could hardly have been concealed from Almagro, since his own quarters were the appointed place of rendezvous. Yet, he adds, with strange inconsistency, there is no good evidence of his having taken part in the conspiracy. And with greater inconsistency he refers to Almagro's letter to the *Audiencia* of Panama, in which he states that, provoked by intolerable injuries, he and his followers had resolved to take the remedy into their own hands, by entering the Governor's house and seizing his person. It is certain, from the intimate relations existing between Juan de Rada and himself, that he must have been aware of the conspiracy, and, indeed, he was the person who chiefly expected to profit by it. And we think it important to point out that never was conspiracy less justified by actual circumstances. No pretence is made by any of those involved in it that the Marquis was responsible for the death of the elder Almagro; and all that they could allege against him was that he had confiscated a portion of his estates, and that he refused to bestow largesses on them, the "men of Chili," who had been foremost in violating his

declare for what purpose they had met ;" and by this promptitude of action overcame their indecision.—"Hist. Gen.," dec. vi., lib. x., c. vi.

* According to one authority, the day on which the attack should be made was still not settled, when a cavalier, named Pedro de San Millan, broke in upon Juan de Rada, exclaiming, "What aileth you? In two hours they will be upon us to cut us to pieces, for so the Treasurer Riquelme has just declared !"

jurisdiction, and had invaded the territory allotted to
him by the Crown. Wrongs of this kind, however hard
to bear, are not to be righted by the assassin's dagger;
while a temperate representation of them to the Castilian
Government would assuredly have obtained redress. But
putting aside the personal aspect of the question, we
have to consider the political bearings of the crime
accomplished by the Almagrist faction. Under the pious
and sagacious rule of Pizarro, the conquered provinces
were rapidly settling down in tranquillity and order.
Their resources were undergoing a swift process of development. New towns were springing up; new channels
of industry were being opened. Commerce was rapidly
extending, and already the ships of busy traders were
beginning to resort to the Peruvian harbours. The conspirators, in their blind desperation, were prepared to
upset this prosperity, this peace, this growing wealth;
were prepared to overthrow the fabric so carefully constructed, though they had absolutely nothing to put in its
place. They had no leader to succeed to the seat of
Pizarro ; Almagro was young and inexperienced, and not
one among the rude, rough cavaliers who formed his
party commanded the confidence or respect of the Spanish
community. The worst consequences of their act were
neutralised by the opportune arrival of Vaca de Castro,
which effected the immediate establishment of an orderly
government; but even as it was, Peru was deluged
for some years with Spanish and Indian blood. Its
progress was arrested, its prosperity seriously impaired
There can be little doubt that the future of Peru would

have been immeasurably brighter and more auspicious if
Pizarro had lived to complete the work in which he was
so actively engaged. The crime of which Juan de Rada
and his associates were guilty was not only a crime against
the individual, but a crime against the State. It was a
deed of murder without justification and without excuse,
and as such Heaven visited it with a severe retribution,
for in less than eighteen months the Almagrist faction
had ceased to exist; on the bloody field of Chupas
(September 16th, 1542) its hopes and ambition were
crushed for ever.

Issuing in a disorderly company from Don Diego de
Almagro's house, the conspirators, with Juan de Rada at
their head, brandished their swords, and raised the cry
of " *Viva el Rey!* Down with the traitor! Down with
the tyrant who has caused the death of the King's
judge!"* It was the hour of dinner, which in those
primitive days took place at noon. Hence there were
but few persons in the streets, and these, with true Spanish
phlegm, observed quietly to one another, "They are going
to kill the Marquis," or, " They are going to kill Picado."
That no one interfered was due, perhaps, to the little
respect which the early Spanish settlers felt for authority,
or to the fact that the Almagrists were well armed, and
known to be desperate men. As they crossed the plaza,
or great square, one of them named Gomez Perez went
round about a little to avoid a pool of water that lay in
his path, whereupon Juan de Rada dashed hastily through
it, and turning fiercely on his comrade, exclaimed,

* Herrera, dec. vi., lib. x., c. 6 ; Zarate, lib. iv.. c. 8.

"What! we are go'ng to bathe ourselves in human blood, and are you afraid to wet your feet in water? Go back, sirrah! you are not the man for the task we have before us."* And he insisted upon his returning.

Pizarro's palace occupied the opposite side of the plaza. It was approached through two courtyards; the entrance to the outer was protected by a massive gate, which might readily have been defended against a hundred men or more. Unfortunately it was open, and the conspirators poured into the inner yard, still raising their cry of blood. There they were met by some of the Governor's Indian attendants, one of whom was struck down, while the others hastened to the house, exclaiming, " Help, help! the men of Chili are coming to kill the Marquis!"

Pizarro had just finished dinner, and was conversing quietly with some of his friends who, after mass, had looked in to pay their respects, and make inquiries after his health. Among these were his half-brother, Don Martin de Alcantara, Velasquez the Alcalde, Don Gomez de Luna, Francisco de Chaves, the Bishop-elect of Quito, and about fifteen of the principal cavaliers of the place. Some of them, alarmed by the din of voices in the courtyard, left the saloon, and hurried down to the first landing on the stairway, to inquire into the cause. No sooner was it revealed to them by the cries

* "Gomez Perez, por haver alli agua derramada de una acequia rodeo algun tanto por no mojarse ; reparó en ello Juan de Rada, y entrandose atrevido por ol agua le, dijo, ' Bamos á bañarnos en sangre humana, y rehusais mojaros los pies en agua ? Ea olveos.' Hizolo volver, y no asistio al hecho."

of the Indians, than they retreated into the house ; and thence, as they were unarmed, by a window that over-looked the gardens they easily effected their escape. Among these prudent gentlemen was the Alcalde Velasquez, who, in order to use his hands in his descent, held his wand of office in his mouth ; thereby, says the chronicler, sharply, being careful to fulfil his assurance to Pizarro that no harm should befall him while he held the rod of justice in his hands ! *

The Marquis, on hearing the nature of the outbreak, preserved his usual composure, and called to Francisco de Chaves, who was in the outer apartment opening on the staircase, to secure the door, while his brother Martin and himself put on their armour. We agree with the historian that if De Chaves had been as calm as his master, and had coolly obeyed the order coolly given, all would yet have gone well, for the door could have been easily held against a stronger force than the conspirators brought with them, until Pizarro's soldiers could have come to his support. But De Chaves, in his impatience or his surprise, half opened the door, and began to parley with the Almagrists, who, throwing themselves upon him, slew him, and flung his dead body down the stairs. For a moment their further progress was stayed by his attendants ; but these, too, were quickly slaughtered, and Rada and his comrades, shout-

* " En lo qual no paresce haver quebrantado su palabra, porque despues huiendo (como adelante se dirá) al tiempo, que quisieron matar al Marques, se hecho de vna ventama abajo á la huerta, llevando la vara en la boca."—*Zarate*, " Conq. del Peru," lib. iv., c. 7.

ing, "Where is the Marquis? Death to the tyrant!"
strode through the hall into the adjoining chamber,
where Don Martin was assisting his brother to put on
his harness.

Don Martin, perceiving that the assassins had gained
the entrance to the apartment, sprang to the doorway,
and assisted by two of Pizarro's pages, and a faithful
cavalier, Don Gomez, sought to beat them back. The
struggle was desperate; though with nineteen against
four, the result could not be doubtful. Two of the conspirators, however, paid with their lives the just penalty
of their bloodthirstiness. But Alcantara and his companions were mortally wounded.

At length, Pizarro, unable, in the pressure of the
moment, to adjust the fastenings of his cuirass, flung it
aside, wrapped one arm in his purple robe, and snatching
up a spear, rushed to his brother's support. Too late;
covered in blood, Alcantara sank swooning to the floor.
The Marquis was now about seventy years of age, but
time had not dulled his courage, though it had impaired
his physical strength. He faced his enemies with a
stern brow and flashing eyes, dealing desperate blows,
while he cried, "What ho! ye traitors and cowards,
have you come to murder me in my own house?" Two
of the assailants fell before him; but the others renewed
the assault, responding to his upbraidings with the
shout of " Down with the tyrant!" The doorway being
secured, Pizarro was able to hold it for some minutes,
until his companions were overpowered, and Juan de
Rada, with a burst of impatience, calling out, " Kill

ASSASSINATION OF PIZARRO.

him ! kill him ! why this waste of time?" thrust one
of his associates, Narvaez, upon Pizarro's spear, and
forced his way into the room. The Marquis defended
himself most gallantly, until receiving a wound in the
throat, he reeled, and fell to the ground. Juan de
Rada and some others then thrust their swords into
the great captain's body. " Jesu ! " he exclaimed, as the
last word he uttered in this life ; and dipping his finger
in his blood, he traced a cross upon the floor and kissed
it. At that moment a base wretch, named Borregan,
dashed a water-jug, which he had snatched from the
table, upon his prostrate head ; and as if this final insult
were too much for his proud spirit, the Conqueror of
Peru fell upon his face and died.*

Waving their blood-stained swords, in that frenzy of
excitement which frequently follows upon the commission of a desperate deed, the murderers rushed into the
street, and raised a loud shout of " Long live the King !

---

* Dr. Robertson's account differs from the text in some unimportant particulars :—" The Governor, whose steady mind no form
of danger could appeal, starting up, called for arms, and commanded Francisco de Chaves to make fast the door. But that
officer, who did not retain so much presence of mind as to obey
this prudent order, running to the top of the staircase, wildly asked
the conspirators what they meant, and whither they were going?
Instead of answering, they stabbed him to the heart, and burst into
the hall. Some of the persons who were there threw themselves
from the windows ; others attempted to fly ; and a few, drawing
their swords, followed their leader into an inner apartment. The
conspirators, animated with having the object of their vengeance
now in view, rushed forward after them. Pizarro, with no other
arms than his sword and buckler, defended the entry ; and sup-

the tyrant is dead! Long live the Governor Almagro! and now shall justice be done!" From all quarters flocked the men of Chili to gather round the banner thus uplifted, until they numbered upwards of two hundred, armed, and ready for the most violent actions. A guard was posted at the houses of the leading Pizarrists, and their persons were taken into custody. As for the palace of Pizarro, and the residence of his secretary Picado, they were immediately pillaged, and a large booty of gold and silver was found in the former. Picado sought an asylum in the house of Riquelme, the royal treasurer, who, however, hastened to betray him, and he was dragged forth, amid shouts and execrations, and flung into prison. The people of the city were sternly bidden to keep within doors. The public treasury was seized, and the wands of office were wrested from the hands of the Alcaldes, who had been appointed by the murdered Governor.

A general feeling of terror pervaded the whole city,

ported by his half-brother Alcantara, and his little knot of friends, he maintained the unequal contest with intrepidity worthy of his past exploits, and with the vigour of a youthful combatant. 'Courage,' cried he, 'companions! we are yet enow to make these traitors repent of their audacity.' But the armour of the conspirators protected them, while every thrust they made took effect. Alcantara fell dead at his brother's feet; his other defenders were mortally wounded. The governor, so weary that he could hardly wield his sword, and no longer able to parry the many weapons furiously aimed at him, received a deadly thrust full in his throat, sank to the ground, and expired."—"Conquest of America," ii., 354-5. Our own account has been carefully put together from a comparison of the various original authorities.

and everybody contemplated with alarm the prospect of a reign of spoliation and cruelty under the dominance of the Almagrists. But, for the time, there was no one to lead an organized opposition. To appease the excitement, and recall the successful conspirators to a sense of decency, the Brethren of the Order of Mary assembled in solemn procession, and bore aloft through the streets the sacred host.

Rada and his followers, however, were content with the victory they had gained, and sheathed their bloody swords. The municipality at their summons recognized young Almagro as Governor, and being set on horseback, he was escorted through the city by his cavaliers, with much enthusiastic shouting and the martial sounds of trumpet and clarion.

For some hours the corpses of Pizarro and his followers lay unhonoured and unnoticed. Some mean spirits there were who would fain have dragged the great conqueror's body to the market-place, and fixed his head upon the public gallows. But Almagro was more generous, and privately granted permission to Pizarro's friends to give it a decent burial. Apprehensive of violence, Pizarro's wife, a faithful attendant, and a few Indians, wrapped the body in a cotton cloth and removed it to the cathedral, where, in an obscure corner, a grave was hastily dug, and by the light of a few tapers the last offices of the Church were hurriedly discharged.*

* A few years later, when order and a settled government were once more established in Peru, the remains of its conqueror and discoverer were deposited in a richly-wrought coffin, and interred in the chancel of the cathedral under a stately monument. Again, in

The obvious reflection to which such an incident gives rise is summed up in the old and bitter words, *Vanitas vanitatum !* History abounds in similar illustrations of the nothingness of human ambition, of the fickleness of what men call Fortune, of the sudden calamity that so frequently overtakes prosperous power. At noon that day Pizarro seemed secure in the enjoyment of almost boundless authority ; millions trembled at his frown ; with liberal hand he could reward the faithful or chastise the presumptuous. Wealth was his, though he did not care to accumulate it ; and fame, though it is probable that this he valued even less. He was master of the vast and affluent territories which he had conquered by the patient and strenuous exercise of fortitude, courage, and capacity. Such was Pizarro at noon ; and yet as the sun sank below the golden rim of the Pacific, a fearful little group of humble followers were huddling his corpse, gashed with many a wound, and streaked with blood, into a secret tomb !

"Such," says the historian, "was the miserable end of the Conqueror of Peru,—of the man who, but a few hours before, had lorded it over the land with as absolute a sway as was possessed by its hereditary Incas. Cut off in the broad light of day, in the heart of his own capital, in the very midst of those who had been his companions in arms, and shared with him his triumphs

1607, when a new and more sumptuous cathedral was erected a second translation took place, and Pizarro's bones were laid by the side of those of the best viceroy whom Spain ever bestowed on Pizarro's conquest, the able and amiable Mendoza.

and his spoils, he perished like a wretched outcast. 'There was none, even,' in the expressive language of the old chronicler, 'to say, *God forgive him!'"* *

We may conjecture that Pizarro was nearly seventy years old at the time of his death ; and though he had lived a life of extraordinary adventure and constant exertion, his eye was not dimmed nor his strength abated ; he retained all the energy and vigour of his youth, all the tenacity and resolution of his manhood. He was never married ; but by an Inca princess of the royal blood, a daughter of Atahuallpa and granddaughter of Huayna Capac, he had two children, a son and a daughter. Both survived him ; though the son did not live to attain manhood. The daughter, Francisca, accompanying her mother to Spain, became the wife of her uncle, Hernando Pizarro, then in captivity at Medina del Campia. This strange and unnatural marriage necessarily received the sanction of the Roman Church. The title and estates of the great Marquis were not inherited by his illegitimate children ; but in the reign of Philip IV., and in the third generation, the Marquisate was revived in favour of Don Juan Hernando Pizarro, who, in acknowledgment of the illustrious services of his ancestor, was created Marquis of the Conquest, *Marques de la Conquista*, and received a liberal pension to enable him to maintain his dignity. It is said that

---

* " Murió pidiendo confesion. i haciendo la cruz, sin que nadie dijese, ' Dios te perdone.' "—*Gomara*, " Hist. de las Ind.," c. 144. Prescott, ii., 170 ; Helps, iv., 141, 142 ; Dr. Robertson, iii., 355 ; Zarate, lib. iv., v. 8.

R

his descendants, still bearing this honourable title—
which recalls the occurrence and interest of a remarkable
enterprise—are to this day to be found at Trujillo, in
the ancient province of Estremadura, the cradle of the
noble family of the Pizarros.

A portrait of the conqueror is preserved in the old
viceregal palace at Lima. He was tall in stature, well-
proportioned, with a striking and attractive countenance,
a natural air of command, and much suavity of address.
Though he raised himself to his high position and pride
of place entirely by the exercise of the consummate
qualities of perseverance, patience, and daring, he filled
it like one to the manner born. The influence which
he exercised over his rude soldiery and independent
cavaliers is extraordinary ; almost alone of Spanish conquerors, he was untroubled by insubordination, and even
Almagro, when in his company, contentedly submitted
to his will. He had none of the Spaniard's usual weakness for splendid dress ; unlike Cortes, his fellow-con-
queror, he had no taste for pomp or pageant ; his usual
costume on public occasions was a black cloak, a
citizen's ordinary dress, a white hat, and white shoes ;
the last, it is said, in imitation of Gonzalo de Cordova,
the " Great Captain," of whose character he was a profound admirer.

He was a man of great moderation in all things ; he
drank but little, and ate sparingly; and he usually rose an
hour before dawn. Capable of great endurance, he shrank
from no amount of labour, and the minutest details of
every transaction received his personal attention. He

has occasionally been spoken of as avaricious, but all the evidence extant seems to point in an opposite direction. Assuredly, he left behind him no accumulated fortune. Whatever he acquired,—and his share of the plunder of Peru was necessarily considerable,—he expended upon public improvements and great architectural works. He was very liberal towards all who served him; and none ever did him a kindness without finding that it was not forgotten. His activity was almost boundless; to the last day of his life he was engaged in public affairs, and during the brief period of his authority in Peru he initiated a thousand useful and practical schemes. Not less conspicuous was his largeness of view; though without culture or even the rudiments of education, he showed himself capable of appreciating the wants of a country and the best methods of developing its resources. But the most distinctive feature of his character, that which marks him out among the great adventurers and explorers of his time, was his constancy of purpose—that tenacity to which I have already alluded—that firm, inexpugnable grasp of the object to be attained, the work to be accomplished. It has been well said that in his first expedition he gave a striking evidence of it among the dreary marshes and mangroves of Choco. Though his followers were pining around him, blighted by the dread malaria, wasting before an invisible enemy, unable to do battle in their own defence, he never faltered, never hesitated; grimly self-reliant, he persevered to the end. And so it was throughout that stormy career, the record of which forms so picturesque a chapter in the history of the New World.

The perusal of that chapter has wrested from a by no means too favourable writer the following testimony :— "When we contemplate the perils he braved, the sufferings he patiently endured, the incredible obstacles he overcame, the magnificent results he affected with his single arm, as it were, unaided by the government,— though neither a good, nor a great man in the highest sense of that term, it is impossible not to regard him as a very extraordinary one." This we take to be the decision at which all impartial judges must arrive.

We append the poet Southey's inscription for a monument at Trujillo :—

> " A greater name
> The list of glory boasts not. Toil and pain,
> Famine, and hostile elements, and hosts
> Embattled, failed to check him in his course ;
> Not to be wearied, not to be deterred,
> Not to be overcome. A mighty realm
> He overran, and with relentless arm
> Slew or enslaved its unoffending sons,
> And wealth and power and fame were his rewards."

www.ingramcontent.com/pod-product-compliance
Lightning Source LLC
Chambersburg PA
CBHW030645030726
47497CB00006B/1958